Fangs, Fur, and Celtic Fairie Tales

A paranormal erotic romance novella collection by
Michelle Houston

MICHELLE HOUSTON

Dedicated to those who believe …

A paranormal erotic romance novella collection by

Michelle Houston

www.unleashedink.com

MICHELLE HOUSTON

Published by Unleashed Ink

TABLE OF CONTENTS:

TIME AFTER TIME

FANGS AND FUR

SANDS OF TIME

Chapter One

Nicole looked at her reflection in the window, wondering when her green eyes had turned so dull and lifeless, while her doctor droned on, and tried to break the news gently that she was dying. As if there was ever a warm and fuzzy way to tell someone they only have months left to live. For some reason, a line from one of her favorite TV shows ran through her head. Something about people thanking a doctor for telling them they have cancer. Pushing aside thoughts of House, mostly because she would be dead before the next season started, she did her best to focus on the slim hope her doctor was so graciously offering.

"With treatments, we could buy you some time, but we'll have to be aggressive with it."

"So, what are you saying? I can stay here, in the hospital half of my time getting poison pumped through my veins, in the hopes that I will live a month or two longer, most of that in pain or throwing up. Or, I can just walk away, and enjoy the time I have left."

"Nicole, I'm sorry, but we caught it too late. There is no way to completely cure you, but we can prolong what time you have."

Shaking her head, she waved the doctor away when he moved to pat her shoulder. Feeling the heat of her tears on her cheeks, she swiped at them with the back of her hand, determined to meet this thing head on.

"I'm sorry, doc, but I can't—I won't—live out what time I have in pain and misery. I'll take the few months I have and do the things I always pushed off for some other day. Well, someday is here, damn it!"

She could feel his sympathetic gaze following her as she opened the door and stepped out of the room. Nurses passed her by, their gazes lowered. Frustrated, Nicole tossed her paperwork on the counter and waited for the clerk to hand her back her forms for her insurance.

"I'm sorry, Nicole, I don't see a scheduled time for your next visit. Let me just call the doctor and ask him when he—"

Nicole cut her off, "Don't bother. There won't be another appointment." Leaning forward, she grabbed her copy of the paperwork from the startled clerk's hand and walked out, the door swishing closed behind her.

* * *

She made the ride home mostly on auto-pilot, turning when her mind reminded her to turn, without any real conscious decision. Her mind whirled with thoughts, each clamoring for attention. Pulling out her cell phone, she debated calling for an emergency pow-wow. Julie was curious by nature, but she wasn't about to attempt to tell her best friend what was going on over the phone. Julie had known she hadn't been feeling well the last few weeks, but she hadn't shared the true trauma of the biopsies—the endless testing and retesting, and the waiting—with her. The bonds of friendship went far, but she wasn't about to drag her vibrant friend down with her, regardless that she would have taken time off of work and sat with her. What she had craved was someone to hold her, when the darkest hours of the night had fallen, and she had lain awake, all too aware of the ticking of the clock. She had raged, had cried, and had been all too tempted to let depression swallow her whole.

Blinking away the tears that threatened to overtake her, she wished for the thousandth time that she had found someone to love, but at the same time she wouldn't wish the misery of watching a loved one die on anyone.

Maybe it was better that she wasn't married, or even seeing anyone. This way, she could go off on her travels, and no one would have to sit helpless while she withered away.

Just as she was about to turn into her driveway, a thought came to her. "I've always wanted to see Egypt. Then there's Scotland, and Ireland. Oh, and I want to visit the Virgin Islands, and spend a few days on the beach."

Driving past her home, she headed back downtown, and turned into the parking lot of

Julie's work. There was something she could do, something that would allow Nicole to tell her what was going on, and let her help without giving her a chance to sink into the depression.

Looking up at the sign for Get-A-Way Travel Agency, she felt some of the shock wearing off. She'd been numb since the results of the biopsy came back, but now she started shivering, suddenly very cold and afraid. She was going to die in four to six months. And it wouldn't be painless, either. The temptation to run out in front of a bus and just get it over with was overwhelming.

As her gaze unfocused, a fresh flood of tears trickled down her cheeks. Stubbornly brushing them away, she squared her shoulders and climbed out of her car.

She was going to go out like she'd lived, on her own terms.

Giving the door a harder shove than required, she stormed into the subdued lobby, catching the attention of the receptionist. "I need to see Julie Anderson, please."

"It will be just a moment, if you'll have a seat. Who should I say is here?"

"Tell her it's Nicole Jeffries, and that it's important."

Sitting still in the chair, very aware of the minutes of her life tickling away, Nicole had to fight the urge to just get up and walk to her friend's office. She was rising to do just that when the receptionist motioned her over. "She'll see you now."

When Nicole popped her head around the corner and knocked against the doorframe, her friend looked up and stood. "Nikki!" she exclaimed. "It's good to see you."

"You, too, Jules. Look, I need a favor. I want to book a trip and I need to do it today."

"Okay, hon, have a seat." Waving a perfectly manicured hand at one of the two overstuffed chairs facing her desk, she reclaimed her seat. "Where do you want to go?"

"I thought that I would start with Scotland and go from there, hitting the truly breathtaking spots."

"Wow. Um, I don't know what to say; this is kind of out of the blue, hon. When do you want to set this up for? Next summer?"

Nicole shook her head, trying to fight to urge to laugh hysterically as her mind taunted her with the reminder that there wouldn't be a next summer for her.

"I want to leave this weekend, and I want the trip to take three months, with hotels and everything booked in advance. You can work on the details for the later spots after I get to Scotland."

"Okay, what's going on?" The concern in Julie's voice was her undoing.

Nicole took a deep breath and tried to put her thoughts into words. She didn't want to break down. She was determined that she make it through the coming conversation with at least some of her dignity intact.

"You uh, you know that I went to the doctor a few weeks ago."

Her friend nodded.

"Well, it wasn't a vitamin deficiency like I told you. They suspected cancer. Today, they confirmed it."

Julie chocked on a sob, her hand pressed hard against her mouth. "When do you start chemo?"

Looking into her friend's eyes as she answered was the hardest thing Nicole had had to do. "I don't. They uh, they can't do anything for me. It's too far spread. I've got less than half a year."

Mentally hearing sand trickling through an hourglass, Nicole had to fight the urge to continue talking, to get it all out and said. Her friend needed a moment to process the bombshell she had dropped in their laps, and she was going to give it to them.

"There's no hope?" Julie's voice broke as she spoke. Reaching out, Nicole covered her friend's hand that was working to shred a piece of paper sitting on her desk and squeezed tight.

"None."

"What are you going to do? Do you have any plans made?"

Nicole bit back a hysterical giggle, and as she laid out her plans, they held onto each other. Nicole knew that for Julie, holding her hand was her only way of controlling things. In the blonde's mind, if she clasped tight enough and willed it so, maybe, just maybe, she could make things change.

Julie nodded with her as she outlined where she wanted to go. "As I said, I want to start with Scotland, hop a plane to England and Ireland, then over to France, down to Italy, and finally stopping in Egypt. From there I want to catch a flight to Japan and end my trip in the Virgin Islands, or some other exotic locale."

Typical of her nature, Julie jumped in wholeheartedly. "I'll need your credit cards. I say let's go for the gold. Five star hotels, first class flights, the works."

Nicole nodded, her throat too tight to talk. She loved this woman, like the sister she never had. And yet, in many ways they were closer.

"You had better keep in touch, and if you start—" Julie's voice cracked and dropped off. She took a deep breath and continued, "If you start to feel weak, you call me, and I'll catch the next flight out. I don't know if you will be back before... before..."

Looking at the sister of her heart, Nicole nodded. "If I know it's coming, I won't try to face it alone, okay?"

"Okay. Are you sure you want to go alone? I could take some time off and we could go together."

As tempting as the idea was, and as frightening as the thought of traveling to several foreign countries alone was, Nicole didn't think she could handle Julie watching her, wondering every day how much longer she had.

"I'm sure. I think it will be better this way. But, I'll send you lots of hokey postcards and souvenirs."

"You'd better." Julie paused to wipe a tear away, then turned her focus back to her computer screen. "S'okay. Let's get that credit card number and get some reservations made."

SANDS OF TIME

Chapter Two

After leaving the travel agency, Nicole headed home and made a list of things she needed to buy for her trip, then another list of things she needed to do before she left, like quit her job. Quitting without notice was actually a fairly painless task, despite having worked there for three years. She then spent the next few days shopping and before she knew it, it was Friday night.

As she lay in bed with her mind racing, she finally gave up on sleep and climbed out of bed. Passing her new luggage as it sat in the hallway, waiting for her to grab it on her way out the door, she headed down the hall to the kitchen and the soothing relief of herbal tea.

While the teapot heated, she pulled a cup from her cabinet and grabbed her tea canister. Selecting the familiar comfort of Earl Grey, she pulled the teabag from its packet and dropped it into her cup.

The teapot chose that moment to start whistling and she grabbed her oven-mitt, careful not to burn herself while pouring the boiling water into her cup.

Sitting at the table, steeping the bag in the water, she finally admitted to herself that she probably wouldn't see her home again. Julie would have to pack her stuff up, donating most of it to the women's shelter and selling the rest. Years ago, fresh out of college, they had gone in together to make out their wills, too aware of the fact they weren't immortal after losing one of their beloved teachers to a car crash. Julie was her executor, and for the first time it sunk in that her friend would have to go through her things, separating out what was of sentimental value to her and what wasn't. Luckily there should be enough money after everything was sold to pay off her debts, including her recent credit card purchases.

Cradling the cup in her hands, she got up from the table and started wandering around her home, trying to see it through someone else's eyes.

The collection of candlesticks her grandmother left her, which she faithfully added to every year on her grandmother's birthday. The plethora of photos of her and her parents, which spanned her childhood up until age eleven, when a boating accident tore them from her young life and her grandmother stepped in to raise her. Her furniture, her paintings and prints, and assorted knick-knacks that turned her apartment into a home…all of it had to be dealt with. It was enough to drive her crazy just thinking about it.

Pushing the thoughts aside, she walked into her bedroom and sat down on the edge of her bed, blowing gently on her tea in an effort to cool it. The heat of the cup slowly seeped into her hands, warming them if nothing else.

It was a long time until dawn broke, a long night of what-ifs dwelled on and regrets compiled.

* * *

The next morning, tired from her sleepless night, Nicole answered the door to find a young man in a chauffeur's uniform. "I'm here to pick up Nicole Jefferies for a ten AM flight."

"That's me," Nicole whispered, stepping back into her apartment. "I'll just get my bags and my purse."

"If you'll show me where your bags are, I can get them for you."

Waving him to her two rolling suitcases, she grabbed her purse and overnight bag and stepped aside. As he grabbed her bags and wheeled them out the door, she turned and looked around her living room one last time, then stepped into the apartment complex hallway and pulled her door shut. Quickly locking it, she followed the chauffeur down to the waiting limo, glad that Julie had made the arrangement instead of trying to drive her herself.

* * *

By the time the plane finally landed at Glasgow International Airport, Nicole had slept some and worried a lot more. Sitting on the plane during the long flight to New York and then waiting for her next flight out to Scotland, she had nothing to do but think. She tried reading a book she picked up at the magazine stand in the busy terminal, but when she flipped to the back of the book there was a big ad telling about the sequel, due out in May of the following year.

Stifling the hysterical laugh that threatened to overwhelm her, she tossed the book onto a seat beside her and left it when the boarding call was announced her flight. There simply wasn't any point in reading it.

Tired beyond imagination, emotionally and physically, she finally slept, spending most of the flight to Scotland in a state without memorable dreams.

As she walked out of the airport, greeted by sunshine in a foreign country, she took a deep breath and worked to push all unpleasant thoughts aside. There wasn't any good to come of dwelling on things—the whole purpose of the trip was to enjoy what time she had left, and she couldn't do that when torturing herself with the knowledge of what would eventually come.

Looking down the line of taxis and limos waiting to take passengers to their destination, a man holding a sign caught her attention. Reading her name, she hefted her overnight back up onto her shoulder and grabbed a suitcase in each hand, precariously wheeling them down the sidewalk.

"I'm Nicole Jefferies," she announced to the gray haired gentleman standing next to a classic Rolls.

"Ah, Ms. Jefferies. I hope your flight was uneventful." Even as he spoke, he was opening the door for her. "Just leave your suitcases on the walk, I'll load them for you."

Slipping into the luxury of the limo, she sank into the plush seat, feeling truly in another world. It seemed Julie had gone all out with the arrangements, sparing no expense to her credit card. As she leaned back against the seat, she closed her eyes and allowed her mind to wander. Before she knew it, the miles from the airport to the castle where Julie had booked her a room had flown by and the car was pulling to a stop.

"We're here, miss."

Her eyelids flickered open, and the wonder that met her gaze had her gasping. The castle was simply breathtaking. Julie chose the location well, even if it had taken over an hour to get from the airport. All she knew before she arrived was that the castle was located on a cliff, and boasted a garden. That description didn't do the castle justice.

As her driver escorted her from the car to the front desk for check in, she struggled not to play the part of gawking tourist. Judging by the subtly amused faces of the castle staff, like many others, she was failing.

The whole checking-in process and being shown to her room passed in a blur. Completely worn out by the events of the past few days, Nicole curled up on the top of the covers, still dressed in her travel clothes—jeans and a comfortable T-shirt—and fell asleep.

SANDS OF TIME

Chapter Three

Nicole couldn't tell what time it was when she woke. It was dark outside, judging by the view outside her window, and she desperately wanted a few more hours sleep, but something was rubbing against her arm.

Batting at it, she brushed her fingers over soft fur. With a squeal, she jerked upright, almost falling off the bed. Looking over the edge, she saw the biggest cat imaginable staring back at her, its golden eyes unblinking. Twice the size of a normal house cat, it was almost solid black, save for a dash of white on its chest.

"How did you get in here?" As she spoke, the cat cocked its head to the side, and continued its unblinking observation of her. Wincing at the kinks in her muscles, she swung her legs off the bed and stood. Her arms lifted over her head, she started stretching; the cat worked its way between her legs, rubbing its head along her knees before jumping onto the bed and laying down.

Wrinkling her nose at the state of her clothing, Nicole stepped into the bathroom and kicked them off, wanting to take a quick shower and change her clothing before exploring. Looking at the cat, she wondered for a moment if she should let him out first, but since he just looked at her

21

and started licking his paws, she shrugged and moved back into the bathroom, where the shower beckoned.

Several minutes later, after the warmth of the water soothed her tired muscles, she reluctantly turned off the tap and climbed out of the shower. Quickly drying off, she wrapped the towel around her and moved into her room. After picking out her clothes, she was about to drop the towel and get dressed when she caught the cat's gaze on her. Feeling oddly shy about undressing in front of it, she shook her head at herself and dropped the towel. As if fluttered down her body it caught briefly on her nipples, sending a shiver down her spine.

The cat's golden eyes followed her movements as she ignored the sudden rush of arousal that coursed through her, stepped into her panties and pulled them up, then quickly donned her bra and slipped into a light dress.

"Well, I suppose you want out." In answer the cat jumped to the floor and followed her to the door, keeping close on her heels as she stepped into the hallway and started down the winding staircase. The clerk didn't seem to notice anything amiss as the cat followed her out the door to the grounds, occasionally winding between her feet as she walked.

Once outside the castle, Nicole drew in a deep breath, the scent of flowers and night air teasing her nose. As her eyes adjusted to the soft light of the light posts, she started along a path, the cat dodging her step.

"I suppose it's not too bad, I guess. Being sick, that is." Feeling strange talking to a cat, Nicole paused. As she glanced down, the cat lifted its head and its golden gaze caught her attention. In the depths there seemed to be an intelligence that prompted her to continue. "I may not have much longer to live, but I get to see things that most people wait a lifetime to see and simply never do. And at least I'm not going quickly, without any time to do those things."

Coming to a bench that overlooked the sea, she sat down. The cat jumped onto the bench beside her, brushing against her side and softly meowing. Even if the cat didn't understand her words, it seemed to sense her emotional state, which was what she really needed.

"I have several months before the cancer progresses too far, several months of traveling the world, seeing its wonders. I just wish I had someone to see them with. Oh, I know, Julie would have come with me. But, it's not the same as cuddling against a warm chest, feeling strong arms wrap around you as you both stare into the beauty of the sea. While I'm at it, I wish I didn't have to die, either, but I guess that old saying about wishes and horses is right."

"I hope for your sake that you're talking into a tape recorder, and not to yourself."

Nicole started, shocked to hear a deep voice some out of nowhere. Quickly standing, she turned to far the tall man who stepped towards her, seemingly separating from the shadows.

"Actually, I was talking to the cat." Nicole waved her hand towards the bench, only to turn and see that the cat had disappeared.

"What cat, lass?" He was close enough now for her to make out his features: soft black hair, long enough to curl around his ears, a strong jaw and nose. Looking into his eyes, she saw a teasing glint in the amber depths. It matched the dimples that winked at her as he smiled. "There's no cat here."

"There was." The breeze chose that moment to blow, and Nicole shivered, crossing her arms over her chest as her nipples hardened, poking at her bra.

As he moved closer, Nicole couldn't help but admire the feline grace of his movements, even as a cautious voice in her head whispered that she was alone in a strange place, with a strange man.

"I should be getting back inside." As she moved to move past his, he reached out and clasped her shoulder, his hand warm and heavy against her skin.

"I dinna mean to frighten ya, lass." As he spoke his voice deepened, his brogue becoming more evident. "My name's Ciaran. I live near here and sometimes I take a stroll through the grounds. 'Tis something peaceful about this castle, the way it stands so majestic on the cliff, watching the waves rush in."

His hand shifted, gliding down her arm to her hand, leaving a trail of sensual fire in its wake. Nicole trembled, her pulse racing as her body awakened, yearning for more of his touch. As his fingers brushed along hers, she found herself curling hers to intertwine with them, prolonging the contact.

"I'm Nicole." Without being aware of it, she had allowed herself to be guided back to the bench. She jerked as she felt the cold stone brushing against her legs as she sat down, Ciaran still holding onto her hand, his thumb brushing over her knuckles.

"A pleasure to meet you, Nicole."

Looking into his eyes, she found herself mirrored there. Her hair fluttered around her face, blown by the gentle breeze coming off of the water. He blinked, shattering the spell that wrapped around her.

Looking away from his steady gaze, Nicole took a deep breath, and simply enjoyed the quiet company Ciaran seemed willing to provide. As she sat there, her hand lightly clasped in his, she found a feeling of peace gliding over her. This country, its inhabitants, and the way she felt since she arrived, was indeed strange, but welcome.

Beneath her, waves crashed against the cliff, trying to pound the stones into submitting to nature's cycle. All throughout the castle, that cycle was at work, slowly chinking away at the stones, turning them to tiny grains to be blown away on the night breeze.

For a moment, she couldn't breathe. She was like the stones, slowly being stripped apart for her return to the Earth.

Ciaran's grip tightened on hers, almost as if he sensed the direction of her thoughts, and she struggled to push away the knowledge that her time was slipping away from her, and simply enjoy the moment.

"Do you believe in things beyond yourself, Nicole?" So softly spoken were his words, she at first doubted that he had said anything at all, until he turned to face her, a question hovering in his gaze.

"If you're asking if I believe in God, I don't know." She was curious at his topic, but willing— at least for the moment—to see where he went with it.

A smile curved his lips, softening his rugged features and sending a dart of warmth from her breast to her core. "I wasn't talking about a higher power, just things beyond what most take to be all there is. This land is ripe with things beyond our understanding. Our history is filled with tales of the Sith and other such otherworldly creatures."

"I stopped believing in fairy tales and knights in shining armor a long time ago, Ciaran." The oddity of their conversation should have worried her, but sitting there in the dark, in a country filled with folktales and stories of a monster in Lake Loch, it just seemed almost expected. "But, sitting here, where time seemed to have almost stopped several hundred years ago, I could almost believe in fairies playing in the forest."

Just then a strange glint fluttered amongst the trees, then flickered out.

"Will-o-the-wisps, lass, what you're seeing there."

Nicole turned to look into his eyes, struck for the first time at the odd shape of his pupils. They were slightly more elongated that normal. A cool chill rushed down her spine, and a curious flitting at the back of her mind warned that things were never going to be the same again. Shrugging it off, she reminded herself that she was dying; nothing could ever be the same again.

"This land is strange indeed, and holds more wonders that you can imagine. But, it takes a brave heart and a willing mind to embrace them." Before she could ask the meaning to his cryptic comment, his head ducked and he lightly pressed a soft kiss against her lips.

SANDS OF TIME

Chapter Four

Nicole was shocked at first by his audacity, but as his lips remained firmly closed, just softly pressing against hers, she leaned into him, taking the comfort he so willingly offered. Running her tongue along the seam of his lips, she swept it into his mouth when it parted.

Determined to embrace the joys of life while she could, she wrapped her arms around his neck, willing to have the fling of a lifetime. His hands smoothed down her body, brushing lightly against the sides of her breasts, before coming to a rest— one against her back, the other against her legs. Shifting towards her, he pulled her into his lap then stood, cradling her against his body.

Dizzy with the desire that sparked wherever he touched, Nicole allowed herself to be pulled into the surrealism of the moment. He carried her just off the path into the woods and laid her down on a blanket of soft moss.

Opening her eyes, she saw the same glints as before flittering among the leaves. Several got close enough that she fancied she saw tiny figures, dwarfed by their wings, dancing on air currents.

Ciaran's lips traced along her neck, his hands now resting on either side of her head, bracing his weight above her. Nicole was aware of a million reasons why what she was doing wasn't smart, but it was overridden by the sheer rightness she felt in his arms. Even if it was just one night, it was worth it to feel more alive than she had in a long time.

And really, she had nothing to lose. Any risk she took by making love to a stranger was outweighed by the fact she wouldn't live long enough to suffer the potential outcomes.

"Nicole," he breathed softly in her ear, his voice husky with desire. She could feel his cock straining against the linen of his pants, where his groin pressed against her hip. His nostrils flared with each breath, as he hovered over her, waiting.

Clutching at his shoulders, she pulled him down to her. He shifted with her, moving gracefully to lie in the valley of her body, his pelvis pressed tight against hers. Through the thin layers of material separating them, she could feel his heat. Her breasts felt tight and heavy, straining to be free of the confines of her bra. Leaning up, she pressed a kiss against his lips, thrilling in the firm feel of his flesh against hers. Nipping at his bottom lip, she rocked her hips slightly, craving the feel of his cock filling the emptiness that existed inside of her--even if only for a few stolen moments.

As she broke the kiss, she gently pushed against Ciaran's shoulders until he shifted slightly back and she could slip her hands between them, to button her dress. Ciaran's eyes twinkled, the tiny flecks of gold in them catching the moonlight as she rubbed her hands over the parts of her body she bared, first her bra covered breasts, then the gentle curve of her stomach.

"Yer a wood sprite then, come to tempt me away to your enchanted glade."

Nicole giggled at his light hearted tone. Pulling the edges of her dress aside, she unclasped her bra and bared her aching nipples to his gaze, conscious of the slight gauntness her body had already started to take. The cancer was taking it toll, and she could see it, even if others seemed not to notice.

"Ah, lass, you have no idea the wonders this country offers, but know that in this moment, you surpass them all." As her gaze lifted to his, she could see the heat flaring in the depths, hot enough to almost scorch her skin.

Sliding her hands down her body, she pulled at her panties, eager to remove them even if she had to tear them off. "Let me, luv," he whispered, his voice sliding over her skin like silk. Relaxing into the grass, she felt him move down, his body brushing along hers as he removed her panties. She lifted her hips, then her feet, silently aiding him.

She expected him to slide back over her, but instead he grasped one of her feet in his hands and started to place soft kisses along the curve of her ankle. Working his way up to her knee, he nipped and nibbled, kissed and licked her skin, until

Nicole writhed like a cat in heat, her body begging to be taken.

Reaching for his, she grasped air as he moved back. "Uh-uh, lass, not just yet."

Frustrated, she slapped the ground and whimpered his name.

"I see we have a wee bit of a temper."

Before she could retort, he leaned in and bit her upper thigh, his teeth lightly scraping along her flesh. Nicole parted her legs wider, her pussy clenching at the sensual assault. Rather than come up her body, he moved back down and picked up her other foot.

For an eternity, it seemed, he lavished the same attention to her left leg as he had her right, until she was ready to scream. Her breasts ached to be played with, and since he didn't seem inclined, she cupped them herself, lightly pinching the nipples.

As they responded, she dared to slide one hand down her body, stroking softly over her stomach and down to the very core of her femininity. Dipping a finger just past her moist lips, she started to flick it lightly over her clit, the tiny bundle of nerves sending sparks of pleasure throughout her body.

Closing her eyes, she simply enjoyed the sensations racing through her, until she felt like she was on the very brink of something wonderful. Then his hands cupped over hers, holding them still.

Her eyes flared open, even as she tried to brush his hands away.

"Ciaran," she pleaded, her voice almost unrecognizable. She had never sounded so breathless before, so needy. With a grin he moved to cover her, his body pressing her into the soft grass. Wrapping her legs around his waist, she held him tight against her, heedless that her pussy was wet and grinding against the front of his linen slacks.

"Ah, lass, you sound so sexy, so devilishly sexy." His lips brushed against her, and she could feel his hand moving between them, unbuttoning his shirt and parting it. He wiggled against her, trying to slip it free, but was unable to. Lifting her hands to his shoulders, she pushed the material down his arms, and together they removed it. His pants were a bit trickier, and Nicole had to relinquish her hold on his hips for him to move back long enough to get out of them. As his nude body was bared to her gaze, she couldn't help the taking a long look at his cock, nestled in a bed of hair. Flushed red, his erection was hard and throbbing with each beat of his heart. As she watched, a pearly drop welling in the slit, and the head flushed into a darker red, almost purple color. With an impish grin, she cupped her breasts, her fingers tugging lightly on her nipples.

Ciaran growled softly, his gaze locked on her breasts as she teased them both.

Slowly, watching the his reaction, especially his cock, she smoothed a hand down her breast to her stomach, pausing to trace around her belly button before drifting daringly close to her core. Stopping just a breath away from her clit, she arched her hips, wantonly offering her body.

Another soft growl spilled from Ciaran's lips before he pounced. One moment he was kneeling between her spread legs, and the next he was stretched over her, pressing so perfectly against her as if he were made for her. Slipping her trapped hands free, she stroked them over his hips until she could grip his firm ass in her hands. She pulled him tight against her as she draped first one leg, then the other, around his waist. His cock nudged against her pussy lips.

Ciaran's hand slipped between them, grasping his cock and slowly guiding it into her as his lips pressed tiny kisses along her collarbone. Arching her neck, she silently beckoned him to kiss there as he sank his cock in an inch. Rocking against him, she sucked him in another inch before he pulled back. She whimpered slightly, her body arching for more.

"Shh, Nicole, I'm not going anywhere."

True to his word, he surged forward, driving into her hard enough that she saw stars. Tightening her grip on his ass, she arched into him, grinding her clit against the tiny black hairs covering his groin. The mat of hair on his chest tickled her nipples, and as he slowly started the ancient rhythm between the sexes, his body surged forward with the sound of the waves, only to quickly retreat.

Lost in the maelstrom of her desire, she didn't at first notice the light night mist turn to rain until the droplets started to splash against her heated skin. Rather than tell him they needed to rush inside, she threw her arms out wide, her fingers grasping at the grass as he thrust against her, his breath harsh in her ear as he groaned.

Deep within her, her body was responding, clenching around his cock, seeking to prolong each intensely sensual moment before his cock slid back. Closing her eyes, she fought to push back her orgasm, even as her body protested. Unable to stand it any longer, she dug her fingers into the softening soil, searching to hold tight to this strange country as her orgasm crashed over her. Her body the rocked beneath the wave, being pounded by euphoria so sweet there were no words to describe it.

Above her, she could feel her lover quicken his pace, his husky voice praising her, telling her with softly spoken words how beautiful he found her. An occasional growl punctuated his words. As he groaned, his hips pumping against her in tiny little jerks, she tossed her arms around him, holding him tight as another orgasm swept over her, pulling them both down under the surge together.

She lay there gasping, filled with the sweetest of sexual releases, the enormity of her actions beating at her mind. Ciaran's arms wrapped around her and he rolled them over, until she lay plastered against his side.

The warm rain continued to fall down, hitting the ground around them and sending up little curls of fog. "That was almost magical," she whispered, feeling deeply that she needed to say something, even as she worried about breaking the spell that seemed to be weaving over them.

"Aye, lass, it was. If you're willing, it will be again."

She lifted her head and braced her arms against the ground, her chin cupped in her palm. "There's something you need to know about me, Ciaran." Nicole started to pull away, determined to tell him why they couldn't have more than a few days together. His firm hands cupped her shoulders, holding her still. As she looked into his amber eyes, she noticed again the irregular curve of his pupil. With each blink of his eyes, it seemed to shift, until it teased against her memory.

"There's something I need to tell you, too. Rather, something I will need to show you. Telling you won't matter much."

"Let me go first, please."

Nicole tried to figure out how to tell a stranger, well, an almost stranger, something she had blanched at telling her best friend. She took a deep breath to gather her nerves and opened her mouth to speak. Ciaran pressed a finger against her lips, the pad of his fingertip brushing along the tiny patch of skin under her nose.

"I know you're dying, lass. But, as fanciful as this may seem to ya, you don't have to."

Nicole jerked back, outraged that he had listened to her conversation with the cat, even if he didn't seem to think there had been a cat. "You had no right!"

Pulling at her dress, she tried to dislodge it from under his frame, but only succeeded in tearing the seams on the damp fabric. Frustrated, and scared to death of dying, she gave in to the emotions that had been bombarding her since the doctor had given her the news.

Curling her legs against her chest, she wrapped her arms around them, laid her head down, and started to cry. She could feel Ciaran wrapping his larger frame around her, his chest hair tickling her back, but tried to ignore him.

"Shhh, lass, shhh. I didn't eavesdrop. You told me you are dying. Don't you remember?"

Sniffling as the absurdity of his clam registered, she lifted her head and glared at him through her veil of tears. "No, I didn't."

"Aye, lass, you did."

Shivering as his warmth left her when he stood, she curled her body tighter even as she found herself unable to look away. When he stood in front of her, he kneeled down, and almost instantly a fine green mist started to swirl around him.

Nicole's eyes widened as it enveloped him, and then disappeared as quickly as it had appeared. When it was gone, where Ciaran had knelt rested a huge black cat, with a white brush of fur on his chest, its golden eyes staring at her, unblinking.

Darkness rushed over her as her mind tried to process what she had just seen, and for the first time in her life Nicole fainted.

SANDS OF TIME

Chapter Five

Nicole struggled to remember what she had been doing as she opened her eyes. The sight of a crackling fire greeted her. Shifting on an unfamiliar bed, she sat up suddenly. Pain exploded in her head.

Almost instantly warm arms wrapped around her, pulling her back against a bare chest. "Easy now, lass, just rest a moment."

Knowing he was right, that her weakened body needed the moment's rest before activity, she still felt compelled to ask, "What are you, Ciaran?"

"Some call me a Cat Sidhe, but the correct term would be Cait Sith. There have been so many legends abound about my race that I have almost lost track of them all, but what you need to know the most is that I am from a race of people who have mixed with humans so long, we might as well be human, save for the ability to shift into a cat from time to time."

Nicole shivered as reality was slowly peeled back. Everything she ever held to be true was systematically shown for a lie. A month ago she would have known beyond a shadow of a doubt that she was healthy, and that save for an accident, she would have many more years of life left to live.

Now she was told that things of folklore existed. It was enough to make her feel lightheaded and dizzy. Ciaran's arms tightened around her, holding her closer to his warmth.

"So, then the folk tales are true?"

"Some of them, Nicole, but not all; many are just stories made up to frighten children into behaving. But, there is some truth to some of the stories. You saw the will-o-wisps tonight, but your mind couldn't process what you were seeing. Now you've seen me change form, becoming...I believe the modern term is were-cat. So, knowing that, believe me when I tell you that I can help you."

"Why would you want to?" Even as she spoke, she wanted to kick herself. If there was some way, short of selling her soul that she could cheat the death that was even now reaching out to claim her, she wasn't going to turn it away. Even if the saner part of her mind told her she was grasping at straws, and that no miracle cure could possibly exist.

"Are you sure you want the answer, lass?"

Nicole nodded, not trusting her voice. She was afraid of what he could say, but she had to know.

"While most of my bloodline is human, much of the instincts of the Cait Sith remains; the ability to shift, the calling of the moon, and the instinct to mate. Like some cats, our people have one mate, and we generally see her in our minds long before she comes to us. I've known about you for almost ten years, since I first shifted. I've known you would be sick, and that I would have to convince you not only to accept my help, but that once cured to stay with me."

"Ciaran, I—"

"Shh, luv, let me finish." Nicole nodded and snuggled against his chest, uncertain why she trusted him as much as she did. He was a stranger, a creature not wholly human, but she felt safe with him. She knew instinctively he would die for her if need be.

"You only have two choices, and you have to choose soon, before you won't be able to. One is that you can walk away, forget that you ever saw the otherworld that bleeds over into this one, and live out what time you have left." Almost unconsciously it seemed, his hands started to stroke over her arms, softly caressing her flesh. Nicole was certain from the way he paused that the other option wasn't going to be perfect, but it certainly beat door number one.

Ciaran continued, his voice rough with emotion. "Or, you can let me heal you, but with it comes a price of its own. You can never go home, for to do so would expose something beyond modern science. You have a death sign hovering over you, and if you return home, miraculously cured, it won't be long before doctors start to wonder how and why."

While the logical part of her agreed that it would indeed happen, her heart screamed at the idea of never seeing Julie again.

"Everyone you know and love has to believe that you died here, without question. No one here knows you are dying, and I have worked hard to gather the paperwork to give you a new identity. But, you have to completely cut all ties."

Nicole blinked at the tears that flooded her eyes. Stubbornly brushing them away with her palms, she turned in his embrace until she was curled against his chest, her gaze catching on the streak of white hair that stood out from the curling black mass that covered his chest. Ciaran's fingertips brushed up and down her back, soothing rather than exciting, as her mind whirled with the decision she had to make.

"How would you cure me?" she asked, her voice muffled by his chest.

"Your myths have one part right, we can make more of our kind with a bite, much like your vampires and werewolves. But, we are only allowed to share the gift with our mates. You will remain perfectly normal, almost completely human, except you will be able to shift into a cat. My bloodline, along with a bit of help from the will-o-wisps, will change some of your molecular structure enough to cause your body to fight off the cancer, rather than let it consume it."

"And I can't even tell Julie goodbye?"

"No, lass, you canna. If she is as close to you as I gather, since she is the one your mind focuses on, then she will know something is up. Your voice will betray you, some hint of hope or sadness at losing her will creep into your words, and she will rush here, wanting answers. Unfortunately, it's all or nothing."

Thinking back on all the memories she had of Julie, all the good times and bad, she knew her friend would want her to make the choice that would save her life. Already, she could feel her will to leave this strange man diminish. There was almost an invisible bond, stretching from her to him, holding her there. The idea of leaving him seemed impossible.

"If I walk away—" Her voice broke and Nicole had to clear her throat before she could continue. "If I walk away, what becomes of you?"

"I go on as I have, hoping you will change your mind before it's too late. Then, when I feel you pass on, and all hope leaves me, I will either take life one day at a time, or I will choose like so many of my kind have before, to join you. But, this isn't about me, lass, 'tis about you."

Trying to imagine a world without Ciaran, even after such a short time, seemed impossible.

"Will it hurt?"

"I dinna know, Nicole. I've only seen the changes done on healthy women. I've been told of cases like yours, and they say it hurts a bit. Less than childbirth, I'm told, but not by much. Your body has to expel its poisons and kill the cancer."

His hand cupped her chin, tipping her face up to his. "I'll be there with you, holding you in my arms. And afterwards, I want to take you to meet

Nessie. She's a bonny lass, for a thousand-year-old lake monster."

Shaking her head at what she believed to be his attempt at lightening the mood, Nicole weighed the options. Her heart heavy, she didn't know if she could accept what he was saying. She wanted to live, to spend her life loving the strange man she had just met, but she didn't know if she could live with the self-doubts that would arise. Would she always wonder if she had chosen the path with him for him, or for fear of dying?

"Okay, Ciaran. I just don't know. I need some time."

"Ah, lass, I canna give you much time, but you have a week, maybe two, to decide."

Almost shyly she wrapped her arms around his neck. "I need some time to think about it. But tonight, tonight I just want to feel. All I've done for weeks now is think, debate, worry and fear. Tonight I want to feel alive."

"Now lass, that I can do. See, I find that I have a wee urge to learn your scent."

As the meaning of his words sank in, Nicole's eyes widened, then closed as he shifted her on the bed and crawled down to nestle between her thighs, lapping at her heated flesh.

Running her fingers though his hair, she arched against him, as the tempo of the rain outside his tiny cottage picked up, drowning out all but the sound of her moans and his words.

"Aye, lass, that's it. Purr for me."

TURNING BACK TIME

Chapter One

Julie knew something was wrong before she picked up the phone. Ever since Nicole had gone off to Scotland on her own, determined to live out what time she had by doing the things she'd always dreamed of, Julie had unconsciously been waiting for her friend to call. Or for someone to call on her behalf. Now, almost three weeks after Nicole had boarded the plane, she had gone insane with worry. Nicole hadn't once called.

"I should have gone with her," she told herself, as she picked the phone up from the cradle. "No news at two am is ever good."

"Hello," she rasped, her voice still husky with sleep, even if her mind was fully awake.

"Ms. Anderson?"

Her eyes snapped open at the grave tone of the man on the phone. "This is she."

"Ms. Anderson, I'm sorry to have to tell you like this, but your friend Nicole Jefferies is dead. She got too close to the cliff and fell. We think it was an accident, rather than intentional. We're still trying to recover her body, but with the current this time of—"

Julie cut him off, "If you don't have her body, how do you know she's dead?"

"I know this is difficult, but—"

44

Despite it being rude, she interrupted again, not willing to give him a chance to say she didn't need to go there. Of course she needed to go. Nicole would have done the same for her. "Look, I'm catching the next flight out."

"Really, that's not necessary."

Without giving him time to continue, Julie hung up. Sitting up in her bed, her blonde hair in wild disarray around her face, Julie felt the warmth of tears on her cheeks. In a move that reminded her so much of her friend, she stubbornly brushed them away. There was no way Nicole was dead, not yet. It already wasn't fair that she only had a few more months left. Fate couldn't be that cruel to take that time away from her.

Not really thinking about what she was doing, she called and left a message on the answering machine at work, letting them know an emergency had come up, then called the airlines. There was a flight leaving in less than three hours, and she was determined to be on it.

Numb with shock, she called a car service and quickly packed a bag without really thinking about it, just throwing a few things into it. Her mind kept repeating the mantra that was keeping her sane, that there was no way Nicole was dead. Not yet, not without her being able to say goodbye.

Ever since her friend had told her about her terminal cancer, Julie had searched the Internet, trying to find a miracle cure, even though she knew one didn't exist. She had called every oncologist she found a listing for, only to get the same answer time and time again. They were sorry, but medical science simply wasn't progressed enough to cure some cancers.

Such bullshit!

A knock on her door startled her out of her inner reverie. Pushing thoughts of what couldn't be changed aside, she hefted her suitcase and headed out her bedroom and down the hall. When she opened the door, a dignified chauffer stood there, his eyebrow raised at her state of disarray. Normally Julie would have been horrified at being seen in wrinkled clothing and without her makeup, even before the sun came up. But the thought that her friend might be dead made all her little idiosyncrasies seem childish.

"Julie Anderson?"

"Yes."

"May I help you with your bag, Ms. Anderson?"

Nodding, she handed the bag over, grateful to be free of its weight. Normally she traveled light, each of her suitcases filled with a specific number of clothes for each day. Tonight she was just hoping she remembered underwear and didn't have twenty shirts. She honestly couldn't remember what she packed.

As she slid into the plush leather seat of the town car, she leaned back and closed her eyes, dwelling on the fact that only a week ago Nicole had left after dropping a bombshell. And now she was gone—forever.

* * *

The ride to the airport passed smoothly, and within twenty minutes of arriving she was seated at her gate, waiting for her flight to be called. It was almost unheard of to get through security so quickly, and now she had plenty of time to dwell. Anxiously tracking the plane's movements on the arrival screen, she waited for the inevitable flight delayed posting, even as she tried not to fidget and betray her nervousness. It would be just her luck that security would find her to be a flight risk, and keep her off the plane.

Given the events of the night, she expected the heavens to open with a fierce thunderstorm, but the sky remained perfectly calm, without a cloud in sight. Catching a glimpse of the almost full moon outside the window, she couldn't help wishing Nicole was right beside her, sharing the view.

Her cheeks hot, Julie brushed at them, wiping the tears away, but fresh ones soon replaced them. She finally gave up and silently sat there in the busy terminal, crying for the loss of her friend, even as in her heart she was determined not to give up on her.

TURNING BACK TIME

Chapter Two

Exhausted after her long flight, Julie stumbled down the walkway into the terminal, her suitcase bumping along behind her. It took every ounce of willpower she possessed to put one foot in front of the other, but she kept going.

Stepping out of the terminal, she inhaled deeply Scotland's fresh air, looking around in awe. These were the same wonders Nicole would have seen, her green eyes looking about, taking in the strange sights and sounds.

Despite the modern times, there was a quality to Scotland that instantly brought to mind the times of old, when men in kilts had fought and died to protect their way of life, their women, and their freedom. She could feel her skin tingling, and imagined how Nicole must have felt, with her strong Scottish ancestry. Scotland called to her, as nowhere else had, not even the Caribbean, where she had always planned to retire.

Forcing herself to get moving, even as she was afraid in her heart of what she would find—or not find—Julie headed to the long line of cabs, waiting for fares.

Selecting one that looked the cleanest, she opened the door and slid her suitcase in. Exhausted from the flight, she climbed into the cab, and leaned back against the well worn seat and gave her destination.

"Ay, lass."

Smiling at the heavy brogue that wrapped around his words, Julie settled back and prepared herself for another boring car ride. What she got, however, was a history lesson. The cabbie, it seemed, was from the general area around the castle, now a rather well known tourist attraction. He filled the hour with tales of the architecture, including bits about Robert Adams, the genius behind the castle.

Despite the passion of his words, he didn't quite do the wonder of the castle justice. As they pulled into the drive, Julie caught a breath. The castle stood like a giant, holding strong again the wind beating at it.

As the car pulled to a stop and Julie climbed out, she could feel the strong breeze coming in off the sea, carrying tiny droplets of water with it. Pushing aside a strong sense of foreboding, she headed up the walkway to the castle and checked in. Rather than waste time, she had her luggage taken to her room and headed back out, determined to get some answers.

By the time she was done meeting with the authorities, she was ready to scream. No one had any answers—save that her friend was dead. She had been seen by several of the locals falling over the cliff behind the castle. They hadn't been able to recover her body.

After hailing a cab back to the castle, she couldn't bring herself to head inside. The connection to her friend was stronger outside. Without being aware of it, she unerringly headed around the castle to the cliff.

Approaching carefully, Julie made certain not to get too close to the edge. As the wind whipped around her it hit her like a punch to the chest— her friend couldn't have survived the fall. She wrapped her arms around her waist, the wailing of the wind drowning out her sobs.

A sense of frantic urgency began to build, propelling her to make her way down the carefully built stairs. She stood on the rocky shore, the waves slamming at the boulders that framed the base of the cliff.

"Nicole!" she screamed, her throat tight with anguish. "I love you!"

Unable to hold herself upright, she collapsed, her knees taking most of the abuse. Pillowing her head on her arms, she continued sobbing, shudders wracking her body.

She startled when a hand brushed her shoulder. "Are you alright, miss?"

As she lifted her head, her gaze met the clearest blue eyes she had ever seen.

"No," she managed, but the sniffling started. Like a kid, she tried to remove her tears with the heels of her hands.

"Here now, luv. Enough of that." Firm hands covered hers, pulling them away before he began wiping her cheeks with a soft handkerchief. "Whatever it is, I'm sure it canna be worth killing yourself over."

"Killing myself? My best friend is dead, but I'm not suicidal."

He nodded his head, sunlight catching on his silver hair as his head bobbed. "The tides coming in and soon all this will be underwater, luv. We'd best get back up the cliff."

Julie allowed him to clasp her elbow and pull her upright. A shaft of lust slammed into her, startling her into pulling away. Ashamed at her elemental reaction to this stranger, especially in light of her friend's death, Julie started up the staircase, determined to get away from him and the temptation he presented, as fast as she could.

"Wait, miss. You'll fall if you dinna be careful."

Ignoring him, Julie continued to climb as fast as her legs would carry her. She was almost to the top when her foot slid on the damp rock and she threw out her arms, trying to gain purchase. A firm weight settled against her back, pushing her forward.

"I've got you, luv. Shhh, I've got you."

Julie trembled as his arms wrapped around her, holding her safe as they climbed the remaining stairs together. The scent of sandalwood from his aftershave wafted from his skin, enveloping her in the masculine scent.

As they reached the top of the stairs and stepped onto the firm soil, Julie turned in his arms, wishing to thank him. She ended up brushing her lips against his chest as he continued forward. Stepping back, she allowed herself to remain in the circle of his arms.

"Thank you," she whispered. Uncertainty whirled inside her.

"You're welcome, luv."

"Julie. My name's Julie."

"Ah. Ceud failte, Julie. I'm Roarke."

"Cud fault?"

"Thousand welcomes."

Looking into his blue eyes, Julie almost felt like she was drowning. His head tipped down, and she knew before he did it that he was going to kiss her, and she couldn't summon the urge to resist. As his lips brushed against hers, she almost swooned.

Her heart picked up its beat, her body awakened from its cocoon. Wrapping her arms around his neck, she arched into his embrace, her body undulating against his as she struggled to get closer. There was something almost otherworldly about him, some spark that resonated within him that proclaimed him to be of this land of wonders.

Her breasts heavy, she pressed them against his chest, her nipples pebbling against the soft material of her shirt. His hands shifted to her ass, cupping her against him.

Instant flames raced over her skin, breeding lust within her veins. A moan escaped, but Julie wasn't certain which one of them had made the sound. As it resonated in the night, her eyes flared open.

She came to Scotland to find her friend, or at least to bring her friend's body home. But instead she found a man she felt an instant connection to. She knew Nicole would want her to pursue the spark between them, but deep inside Julie felt like she was betraying her friend by being there with him so soon after her death.

Jerking back like he had scalded her with hot water, she almost relented as his warm hands clasped her upper arms, pained surprise in his eyes.

"I have to go. I'm sorry, Roarke." Stepping back, she held out her hand to hold him still. "Please, I can't do this."

Pressing her hand against her lips, she turned and fled. As she walked away, she could feel him watching her, his light eyes locked on her until she disappeared around the bend.

TURNING BACK TIME

Chapter Three

Booked in the room she'd reserved for her friend, Julie spent a sleepless night tossing and turning, her thoughts in turmoil. Already she could feel a strong attraction to Roarke, a strange urge to rush into his arms and let him push the pain of losing Nicole away, if only for a little while.

Frustrated at her thoughts and her body's betrayal, she tossed the covers aside and climbed out of the bed.

Ruffling her light blonde hair, she headed into the bathroom for a quick shower. Face devoid of any makeup for the first time in years, she caught her gaze in the mirror as she stepped out of the shower, her face still pink from the heat of the water. Her eyes caught her attention. After her rocky divorce, she decided that no man would ever put that haunted look back in her eyes, but after a brief meeting the stranger on the shore had.

She felt cast adrift, and knew meeting Roarke only accounted for part of it. A heavy dose of guilt weighed on her, slowly eating at her. She was alive, and her friend wasn't. The only human being who truly knew her, and who she truly knew was gone, leaving an incredible void. Roarke offered a brief solace, but she couldn't use him like that.

Turning away from the taunting reflection of herself in the mirror, she headed into the bedroom and quickly dressed. She planned to go exploring, and mourn her friend in the country Nicole had always wanted to visit. She had put it first on her list of places to visit when she found out about the terminal cancer because she wanted to make sure she saw it.

After donning a pair of jeans and a t-shirt, she opened the bedroom door and almost tripped over the biggest cat she'd ever seen. Its green eyes started up at her, unblinking as she stepped around it, intending to slip past.

With a throaty meow, it stepped in front of her. Crouching down, she scratched behind its ear, the feel of its soft fur tickling her palm. "You're spoiled, aren't you? You probably have all the staff wrapped around your little paw."

The cat cocked its head, and sniffed the air. Without giving it much thought, Julie picked up the cat and settled back on the bed, holding the creature in her lap. Stroking her hand along the sleek fur, she struggled to hold back the tears that were once again threatening to overwhelm her.

"You're such a pretty cat. I wonder, did you meet my friend Nicole? She would have loved you. She always wanted a cat, but didn't want to have one until she could be home more often." Burying her face in the sleek black fur, Julie allowed her tears to fall, needing the cathartic release.

"I met someone last night, and God above, I don't know why I wanted to jump him. I feel like I lost half of my soul, facing a life without my best friend, but I don't feel the emptiness I should. Something is telling me that she's still alive, and I don't know if it is hope or denial. So when this strange and intriguing man basically saved my life, I wanted nothing more than to toss him to the group and let him push my pain away, even for a little while." Sniffling, Julie wiped her tears against the soft fur as the cat purred in her arms. "I'll bet you can understand that urge, can't you, pretty one? I know Nicole would have."

Unable to stand her pity party any more, Julie determinedly pushed herself off of the bed and set the cat gently on the floor. A series of meows from behind her had Julie turning around to find another black cat, this one with deep amber eyes, standing there waiting. The green eyed cat blinked owlishly, then stepped away, following its companion out of the room and down the stairs. After a quick visit to the bathroom to repair her face, Julie squared her shoulders and headed out of the room, determined to see the Scotland of her friend's dreams. She was going to embrace life for the both of them, so that when she saw Nicole again, which she firmly believed she would, she would have stories to tell her. A click flick of the knob to check and make sure she locked the door, and she headed down the stairs to the lobby.

Julie waved at the concierge as she passed the front desk and headed out into the sunshine. Inhaling the moist air, she found her gaze drawn to the edge of the woods by the castle. Silhouetted against the trees stood a figure.

Strangely familiar, Julie hesitantly started forward. As she moved forward, the features figure became clearer, until she knew she was staring at Nicole. Specter or alive, she didn't know, but her beloved friend was standing there.

Breaking into a run, she had to get across the glen separating them, but Nicole stepped backwards into the tree line, melting into the shadows.

"Nicole!" she yelled, hurrying after her friend.

As she rushed into the tree line, limbs tore at her clothes and hair, but she continued headlong forward until she came to a small clearing. In the middle stood the green eyed cat from earlier.

"Where did she go?" she asked the creature, her eyes scanning the nearby trees looking for some clue as to where Nicole went. Turning around, she came full circle, until she faced the cat again.

"Julie!" A masculine voice called out. Julie shivered as her body recognized the familiar timbre of the man she had met the night before. "Julie, come out of there. 'Tis dangerous in the woods, luv."

As he crashed around behind her, Julie stood her ground, staring into the strangely familiar gaze of the cat. It slinked its way forward, its body moving with a clumsy gait, like a newborn foal.

"Are you hurt, girl?" she asked as she crouched down, holding her hand out for the cat to sniff.

"Julie. Back away, luv."

"It's okay, Roarke. We met at the castle."

His hand clasped her shoulder, pulling her backwards. "It's not the female that has me worried."

A hissing sound echoed through the underbrush, and then the male stepped out, the hair on his back bristling. A stark white patch of hair on his chest gave him a dangerous look.

He stepped between the green-eyed cat and Julie, his amber gaze watchful. Edging backwards, Julie slowly stood, her eyes watching the cat for any sign of danger.

"He was nice enough in the castle, Roarke. What's gotten into him?"

"Just come away, luv."

As she watched, the male nudged at the female, and got swiped across the leg for his troubles. Adding her hiss to his, she stepped around him and a mist began to swirl around them. Blinking, Julie tried to keep the sparkling dust out of her eyes, but her efforts were in vain.

When she cleared her eyes, Nicole stood before her, clad in a simple cotton dress.

"Nikki?" Julie couldn't believe her eyes. Behind her friend stood a tall man, the hair on his head and body as black as sin, save for a white patch on his chest visible because the linen shirt he wore was unbuttoned. Simple cotton trousers covered his lower body.

"Jules, I ..."

"They said you were dead," she cried and rushed into her friends embrace. Crying and laughing at the same time, she held the slender brunette against her, unwilling to let her go.

She wasn't sure how long she stood there, her shoulders shaking with emotions that threaten to overwhelm her when a cleared throat drew her back.

"She is dead, at least as far as anyone back home can know."

Julie's eyes widened at the dark haired man's words. Roarke shifted position behind her, throwing an arm around her shoulders and pulling her into the warmth of his body, while she trembled.

"I don't understand." She wanted to plead with her friend to come home, but something was different about the brunette. She had a vitality to her she had lacked for months. Seeing the sudden change brought home the fact she hadn't noticed her friend was truly ill until Nicole told her, and by then it was too late.

"What did you see here? Honestly, without any hesitation." Ciaran's voice betrayed him, even as his face would have won a poker game. He was nervous, yet curious about her answer.

"I saw..." Julie closed her eyes as she tried to put it all together, just what she had seen. She had seen her friend, then a cat in the clearing, and then after a mist appeared, the cat disappeared and her friend stood there again. Her eyes flew open in shock as it registered. She had been too shocked and gleeful before that Nicole was alive to register the small details.

"I saw Nicole, then a cat, then Nicole again ... but I don't understand ..."

Nicole reached out and clasped Julie's hand and sat on the ground. Her body limp, Julie allowed herself to be pulled down. Her friend's green eyes teared up as she leaned back against her dark haired man as he sat behind her.

"Julie, meet Cairan. Ciaran, this is Julie. My friend and sister of my heart, and the one person in the world I can't keep my secret from. I tried. Julie, please bear with me and I'll try to explain."

Her mind whirling, Julie leaned back against Roarke gratefully as he knelt behind her. Strangely comforted by the silver haired man's touch, she relaxed against him, his hands soothingly stroking up and down her arms.

"When I arrived in Scotland, I knew I was dying. There was nothing I could do about it, and I was determined to enjoy what time I had left. When I met Ciaran, I jumped at the chance to make love to him, to feel alive. Then I found out that he is a Cait Sith, a were-cat. And that he could cure me."

"Cure you? Wait a minute ... he says he's a shapeshifter?" Despite her practical nature, Julie had always been more given to flights of fancy than her friend. Nicole had been grounded firmly in science and things that it could explain. Yet, she couldn't really deny to herself what she had seen. Nicole had changed shapes in front of her.

"Please." Nicole held up her hand, a signal Julie recognized. Her friend was asking for her to shut the hell up, without being rude about it. She could feel a smile curving her lips in response. Just a few weeks ago she would have stuck out her tongue, and Nicole would have swatted at her.

What a difference a few weeks made.

"Cairan told me he could cure me, but it had a price. Since the Sidhe races are trying to stay outside of the notice of scientists who'd want to dissect them, no one could know I had been miraculously cured. No one."

Hurt at the insinuation she wouldn't have kept her friend's secret, Julie couldn't hold back the burst of pain. "I wouldn't have told anyone. Jesus, Nicole!"

As her friend obviously struggled for words, her lower lip trembling, Ciaran spoke up. "My people are few and growing fewer each generation. There are also other races at stake, besides my own. You might have had the best intentions, but someone would have guessed that things weren't as they seemed when you never mourned for your friend. It would have come out, somehow, that

61

Nicole was alive. We, I, couldn't take that chance. She had one choice—live, but let everyone thing she was dead, or she could walk away and slowly die."

Chastened, Julie could only nod. Her throat tight, she struggled to put her emotions to words. "I'm glad you chose life, Nikki. Even if I wasn't supposed to know."

Nicole shrugged, her eyes welling with tears. "I guess I always knew you wouldn't fall for the 'I fell off of a cliff' story. And that you would come searching for answers. I planned to let you leave without telling you, but when I saw you crying, I just couldn't do it. I couldn't be the one to cause you pain."

TURNING BACK TIME

Chapter Four

Julie nodded in understanding. She had never been able to tolerate seeing her friend in pain either, often promoting some of their more daring escapades as she strove to take her friend's mind off of crappy boyfriends, bosses from hell, and the other assorted unpleasant and emotionally painful moments in her life. So she fully understood the why.

"So, you're cured now? You'll be okay?" She could hear the hope in her tone, and knew that Nicole had made the right choice. She wouldn't have been able to play the mourning friend knowing that Nicole was still alive. Already her heart was filled with emotion and the pain of knowing she was going to have to live her life without her best friend.

"Yeah, I'll live. But, I can't go back to my old life."

Julie nodded even as the pain of Nicole's words threatened to tear her apart. Turning to the man holding her, she asked, "What part do you play in all this?"

Roarke sighed, his heated breath ruffling her hair. "My race has as much to lose, if not more than Ciaran's, if word of Nicole's cure gets out."

Julie arched an eyebrow, her mind quickly running through the options—vampire, werewolf, alien, and a plethora of other creatures from myth to folklore. Unable to pinpoint any idea what he could be, she was forced to ask, "Your race?"

"I'm a Selkie, luv." Her puzzlement must have shown, because he continued. "We secrete a coating of fur as we shift into the form of a seal. When we shift back, the fur falls off in a pelt, which is where many legends about my kind originated. Basically, I am a were-seal."

Unable to process the revelations bombarding her, Julie stood and ran an agitated hand through her hair. "So, I'm the only human being here."

"Yes," Nicole nodded, her green eyes grave, "and I know it's asking a lot of you. You've always wanted to believe such things exist, but now that you know you can't tell anyone. I know it's unfair to you, what I did, but I want to live!"

Julie jerked her head in a nod. "I know and I don't blame you. It's just the knowledge that I will go home and try to get back to my life, without ever being able to see you again. I need time to think, to process all of this. Please...I just need time."

Nicole stood and enfolded her in her slender arms. Julie had never been more aware of her friend's fragile strength than she was at that moment.

"Take all the time you need, Jules. Roarke knows where to find me."

Tears hot on her cheeks, Julie pulled away and walked off, leaving the three shape-shifters standing there, talking amongst themselves.

∗ ∗ ∗

Several hours later, Julie headed back down to the shore, seeking the solace that the sound of the crashing waves offered. She'd been unable to think in her bedroom, instead pacing like a caged animal until she felt like she was going to lose her mind.

Selecting a boulder to sit on, she climbed up and drew her knees against her chest, wrapping her arms around them. Resting her chin against her knees, she stared off into the water. The ebb and flow of the waves as they surged mirrored the turbulence of her emotions.

She struggled to process the mind-blowing news that not only was Nicole alive and well, but that she had become a were-cat. Added to that was her attraction to Roarke, the were-seal. She wasn't certain if she could take any more surprises—the last few weeks had dished out enough.

As if her thoughts had conjured him, Roarke spoke from behind her. "Hello, luv."

Julie looked over her shoulder and watched Roarke approach. Unlike Ciaran's feline grace, Roarke moved with a sensual gait, his sleek muscles flexing with each step as he glided across the shore.

"Hi, Roarke."

"Mind if I sit down?" The thought of his arms around her, and where their being alone might lead, sent a shiver through her. She could indulge her passion without guilt now, but she wasn't certain she should.

"Feel free." After waving to a spot beside her, she waited until he joined her, the heat of his thigh brushing against hers, before she turned her gaze back to the water.

Trying to distance her emotions from the compelling man beside her and focus on the problems she had at hand, Julie spoke her thoughts aloud. "Have you ever had the foundation of your world so shaken that you couldn't figure out where to start rebuilding?"

Roarke was silent for a moment. "Twice."

Julie turned on the rock so that she could look into his light blue eyes. His sleek features drew her attention, from his high cheekbones to the slender blade of his nose, which gave him an aristocratic air.

"When?"

His eyes darkened with pain, his words softly spoke. "The first time was when my mother died. I came home from college to find that a drunk driver had hit and run her over as she walked home. She never had a chance."

Julie wrapped her arm around his waist, silently offering him comfort.

"And the other time?"

"Some of the Sith and other related creatures have a lot of the instincts from the animal they shift to, others are very tuned into the universe. Cairan saw Nicole in his dreams years before she arrived here. He knew she would be ill and that there was a chance he could lose her."

Roarke tipped his head and pressed a soft kiss against her lips, startling her. He pulled back before she could respond. "Selkie know our mates when we see them. It is like an electrical charge racing through us and we just know. I felt that charge when I saw you lying on the boulder, crying your eyes out. I knew I would do anything in my power to make your pain go away."

"Mate?" She shook her head in protest. Just when she started feeling normal again, he pulled the rug out from under her. "No... I have to go home in a few weeks."

Roarke cupped her chin in his hand, his thumb softly tracing over her lips. "You will do as you must. Just as I canna deny what I feel."

The soft glide of his thumb sent a shiver of sensual awareness through her. She could see his nostrils flaring in response.

"I want you, luv. But, I dinna want you to have any hesitancy about me, or about us. So I'll wait until you're ready."

Julie licked the seam of her lips, brushing her tongue along his thumb. His eyes widened, the color lightening until his eyes resembled the Caribbean waters—light crystal blue. Leaning forward, she pressed her hand against his chest, feeling his heart beat. Despite the differences between their races, they were very much alike.

"I don't know if I am your mate, but I do know the attraction is mutual. And if I have learned anything from recent events, Nicole's cancer diagnosis, believing she's dead, and finding her alive and in love with someone she just met, it's that you take what life offers if you can." She wrapped her arms around his neck, sliding closer to him until she could climb into his lap, straddling him. "Life's too short for regrets and wasted opportunities. I want you—very much, but I don't know what the future holds. All I know is that for the present, being with you feels right."

"Ah, Julie," he whispered as his lips pressed against hers, "I'm so verra glad you feel that way, lass. Verra glad." His brogue thickened as he spoke, until she almost couldn't understand him. Then his lips began tracing down her neck, pausing to kiss her pulse, and she found herself incapable of speech.

His hands cupped her hips, holding her tight against him as he slid off of the boulder. Surefooted on the rocks, he walked them to the shoreline, all the while kissing along the slender column of her neck.

"Roarke, what..." She gasped as he set her down, the water curling around her feet.

"Trust me, luv. You'll like this." He knelt before her, uncaring of the water lapping around his legs, and started undressing her. Peeling the jeans down her legs, he tossed them on top of a nearby rock, and began slowly pulling her T-shirt over her head, kissing the patches of skin that were revealed an inch at a time. Her shirt soon joined her jeans, and he worked his way back down, pressing soft kisses along the lace edge of her bra.

"That tickles!" She gasped as he delved his tongue into her belly button. She reached behind her and unclasped her bra, baring her breasts to him. The heat of his gaze as his eyes trailed over her weakened her knees.

The cold water continued to pulse against her feet, a startling contrast to the heat of his tongue as he laved attention on her breasts, now freed from her bra. She clutched at his shoulders, holding herself steady when he hooked his fingers in the waistband of her panties and pulled them down her legs, removing the last barrier between her and his questing tongue.

With a wicked grin, he started to move farther south, nipping at the skin on her hip before continuing his journey. As his tongue licked against the smooth shaven skin of her mound, Julie's legs buckled and she knelt on the rocky beach.

Roarke quickly pulled his skirt off and spread it on the ground. While he stood to remove his pants, Julie shifted to lay on the shirt, grateful of the cushion between her skin and the ground.

Although most of the stones were smooth and rounded from the water beating at them, they still felt harsh against her feet.

Bending her legs, she parted them, opening herself for him. Roarke groaned as he unzipped his pants and let them fall. Then it was her turn to moan. Roarke's cock pressed against his underwear, tenting the material in such a delicious way she licked her lips in anticipation.

Holding out her hand, she pulled him down into the cradle of her body and whispered, "Ceud failte."

Roarke's grin lit up his face. "Ah, luv, such sweet words."

As he shifted his hips, his cock brushed against her clit and Julie moaned. Wrapping her arms around his neck, she pulled him down for a kiss as the waves crashed around them. Lifting her feet out of the water, she hooked her ankles together around his back and arched beneath him, coaxing his cock against her pussy.

Roarke shifted his hips, slowly sliding up and down her cleft. Julie dug her nails into his back as her pussy contracted, begging for deeper contact.

"Roarke," she whimpered, arching against him. "Stop teasing."

In response, he reached between them and guided his cock against her pussy, slowly slipping the head past her lips. Julie moaned and wiggled her hips, undulating beneath him as he thrust deeper, joining their bodies.

Shifting her hands to his shoulder, she dug her nails in, leaving tiny crescents in his skin as he started to grind against her, withdrawing and thrusting, falling into an instinctive pattern of mating between two animals.

Breathless, Julie held on tight to him as her body responded with a riot of sensations. The tide came in, waves lapping at her hips, brushing against their lower bodies. Julie squealed at the sudden rush of cold against her heated skin.

Roarke tightened his grip on her hips, pulling her up into his thrusts. Julie buried her face against his neck, her teeth nipping against his soft skin. Roarke groaned as she bit harder, her teeth scraping along his neck as she worked her way to his earlobe. Holding the lobe between her lips, she gently tugged, her tongue rasping against the lower edge. He responded with a hard thrust, driving deeply into her, his cock creating a delicious friction within her.

Locking her legs tight, she squeezed her slick inner muscles around his cock, holding him tight within her. His cock spasmed, and her body responded with a soft flutter within her core. She could feel her orgasm building as he slowly guided her higher and higher with each stroke of his cock.

The waves continued to creep upon them, tickling her ribs as they made love. Relishing the contrast, she arched her back, pressing her breasts harder against the soft mat of silver hair covering his chest. Each breath he took shifted his chest against hers, further teasing the tight little buds of her nipples.

"Roarke." She gasped, helpless to fight the power of her reaction. She wanted it to last an eternity, but she was building to an orgasm too quickly. He whispered against her neck, his breath rushing over her skin as he coaxed her higher. She couldn't tell what he was saying, but his voice was rough and deep, betraying his own building desire.

Unable to hold back, she clenched tight around him as she cried out her release. Screaming his name with her orgasm, her body milked his cock, arching against his rapid thrusts as he picked up his pace. Moments later, he poured his passion into her as he climaxed, his body jerking against her. With a soft groan he collapsed against her, his heart thudding against his chest.

Stroking her hands up and down his back, she basked in the warm afterglow of her orgasm, only to be drawn back to reality as the water reached the outer curve of her breast. Shuddering at the sudden cold, she started trembling and burrowed into the warmth Roarke radiated.

Her body mourned the loss of his as he pulled back and stood. Holding out his hand, he pulled her up and then cupping her hips he lifted her to sit on the boulder next to his clothing.

While he dressed she watched him, admiring the flex of his muscles as he donned his pants and now damp shirt. Pulling her own T-shirt over her head, she was grateful he had thought to keep her clothing dry.

"Roarke, I …"

"Shh, lass. There's time enough to talk later."

After she finished dressing, he lifted her into his arms and carried her back up the stairs to the castle.

TURNING BACK TIME

Chapter Five

For the first morning since learning of Nicole's condition, Julie awoke refreshed. She and Roarke ordered in room service, and spent the evening feeding each other choice delicacies while exploring each others bodies. She had fallen into an exhausted sleep held tight against his chest, her body warmed by his.

In the soft morning light, she watched the gentle rise and fall of his chest as he continued to sleep. Propping her chin in her hand, she laid there, enjoying the simplicity of the moment until his breathing changed and his eyes flickered open.

"Morning," she whispered, uncertain what else to say. It had been a long time since she had fallen asleep in a man's arms.

"Mmmm. Morning, luv." As a soft smile curled his lips, Julie felt a bubble of joy well within her. He made her feel cherished, and very much alive.

Laying her head back down on his chest, she listened to the steady thump, thump of his heart as he stroked his fingers through her hair, gently combing out the tangles.

"Nicole is going to want to see you today."

Julie circled her fingertip around in his chest hair, trying to hold on to the moment. "I know. But I don't know what to tell her."

"Ah, luv. You dinna have to tell her anything. Just be open to considering whatever she proposes. I know I wouldna mind you staying."

She lifted her head and looked into his eyes. Already the sight of him was becoming dear to her. Her heart clenched at the idea of never seeing Nicole again. But, the idea of being separated from Roarke stole her breath away.

"I'll think about it."

"That's all I ask, luv. Besides, there are so many wonders I can show you, so many things that exist which defy your wildest imaginings."

Julie pressed a soft kiss against his chest, then rubbed her face catlike against his skin. "Oh, like what?"

"We'll there's my people, for starters. Then we could move on to the banshee, or maybe Nessie. Ciaran calls her a bonny lass for a lake monster." Julie quirked an eyebrow at him and pulled the sheet off baring his body to her view. Pressing another kiss against his chest, she started to work her way down, kissing along the arrow of fine hair that trailed down to his groin.

His stomach contracted as she brushed a kiss against it. "Go on."

"Or we could, oh, visit Japan." His breath hissed out as she nipped at his belly button. He continued through gritted teeth "They have some interesting folk legends that I wouldn't mind exploring. Then there's always Italy, or England, France, or even ..." his voice trailed off as she wrapped her lips around the head of his cock.

"Or we could decide all that later, luv. Mmmmm, yes lass, just like that."

* * *

AUTHOR'S NOTE

When these stories were originally written, way back in 2007, it was because of a call for stories with a Celtic theme. I wanted to go with something from folklore, and have a little bit of fun with it.

I love the concept of shape-shifters. Partially because the scientist in me wonders about the whole process by which it would even be possible. Also, it is because of the ability to bring animal characteristics into my characters.

So for these stories, I went searching for folklore that could be modified to involve shape-shifters. Obviously, I took my own spin on some things, and didn't stay completely true to the original folklore stories.

Just for fun, I have included some of the research tidbits that I found. I also have the sites I found them on. Keep in mind that time has gone by, so some of the url's might not exist anymore.

Note - I am claiming NO copyright to the following passages and information. I am only sharing my research findings.

~ * ~

Cait Sith

A supernatural cat from the Highland region, the creature was as big as a dog and completely black apart from one white spot on its breast. Perhaps the belief is related to some of the mystery black cats that have been caught in the region.

Selkies

Seal spirits who could take human form on land. They often intermarried with mortals.

http://www.mysteriousbritain.co.uk/folklore/scottishfolkapp.html

~ * ~

Sídhe (IPA [ʃiː], shee, Modern Irish: sí) is an Irish word referring first to earthen mounds that were thought to be home to a supernatural race related to the fey and elves of other traditions, and later to these inhabitants themselves. There are a number of different types of these creatures: aes sídhe, bean sidhe, leanan sidhe, sluagh, cat sidhe, cusith, the fairy host (an slua sidhe) or Wild Hunt, sídhe who can fly through the air and shift shape at will, sídhe who walk the earth at dusk, the guardian sídhe of the lochs of both Ireland and Scotland and many more.

The guardian sídhe is often considered a ghost or half ghost. This is a bit different than the "undead" concept. The sídhe are extremely beautiful and while seem mature, look very young in the face and appear in a different light. The banshee or ban-sídhe is the flying type. Many in the legends are female.

http://en.wikipedia.org/wiki/Sidhe

~ * ~

Cat Sidhe or Cait Sith (pronounced caught shee) is a fairy creature from Celtic mythology said to resemble a large black cat with a white spot on its breast. It was said to haunt the Scottish Highlands. Some common folklore suggested that the Cait Sidhe was not a fairy, but a transformed witch.

The myths surrounding this creature are more common in Scottish Folklore, but a few myths originate in Irish folklore as well.

This comes from the root words "Cait", which meant "Cat" in both Irish and Scottish Gaelic, and Sidhe, which is the word for faery folk or other otherworldly beings.
It is possible that the legends of the Cait Sidhe were inspired by sightings of a rare breed of cat, known in modern times as the Kellas Cat.

http://en.wikipedia.org/wiki/Cat_Sidhe

~ * ~

The Kellas Cat, referred to in Celtic mythology as Cait Sidhe, is a black feline larger than a common house cat, but much smaller than a big cat. It is named after the village in Morayshire where it was first found in 1984, when a gamekeeper named Ronnie Douglas shot and killed one. Before then they were usually thought of as mythological, the few sightings dismissed as hoaxes.

The Kellas cat is described as being over 25 inches long, with powerful and long hind legs and a 12-inch tail, though some claim the tail is shorter. A specimen is kept in a museum in Elgin, Moray.

Some people believe that the Kellas Cat is an unclassified species, or at least a subspecies of the European Wild Cat. However, eight specimens were collected and analyzed by Dr. Andrew Kitchener of the Royal Scottish Museum. He found that seven of the cats had traits of both house cats and wild cats, suggesting they are most likely hybrids.

http://en.wikipedia.org/wiki/Kellas_Cat

~ * ~

Selkies (also known as silkies or selchies) are mythological creatures in Irish, Icelandic, and Scottish mythology that can transform themselves from seals to humans, where "selkie" is simply the Orcadian word for "seal". The legend apparently originated on the Orkney Islands.

Selkies are able to transform to human form by shedding their seal skins and can revert to seal form by putting their selkie skin back on. Stories concerning selkies are generally romantic tragedies. Sometimes the human will not know that their lover is a selkie, and wakes to find them gone. Other times the human will hide the selkie's skin, thus preventing them from returning to seal form. A selkie can only make contact with one particular human for a short amount of time before they must return to the sea. They are not able to make contact with that human again for seven years, unless the human is to steal their selkie's skin and hide it or burn it.[citation needed] The Grey Selkie of Suleskerry is a ballad typical of the former, while The Secret of Roan Inish is a movie telling the latter tale. Seal Child is a children's novel by Sylvia Peck which details a modern telling of this myth. The Folk Keeper, a "young readers" novel by Franny Billingsley also uses the selkie myth powerfully. The recent album "Honeycomb" by Pixies front-man Frank Black includes a tune called "Selkie Bride", which alludes to the Selkie legend.

Male selkies are very handsome in their human form, and have great seduction powers over human women. They typically seek those who are dissatisfied with their romantic life. This includes married women waiting for their fishermen husbands. If a woman wishes to make contact with a selkie male, she has to go to a beach and shed seven tears into the sea.

If a man steals a female selkie's skin, she is in his power, to an extent, and she is forced to become his wife. Female selkies are said to make excellent wives, but because their true home is the sea, they will often be seen gazing longingly to the ocean. If her skin is found she will immediately return to her home - sometimes, her selkie husband - in the sea.
Sometimes, a selkie maiden is taken as a wife by a human man and she has several children by him. In these stories, it is one of her children who discovers her sealskin (often unwitting of its significance) and she soon returns to the sea. The selkie woman avoids seeing her human husband again but is sometimes shown visiting her children and playing with them in the waves.

http://en.wikipedia.org/wiki/Selkies

UNNATURAL BONDS

Kali stared at the unconscious man strapped to the bed and tried not to let her turbulent thoughts show. She'd worked months to get this close to the heart of the research, had given up too much, to lose it all now by being overeager.

"Fascinating, isn't it?" His warm breath blew over her skin like acid, and she wanted to draw away. Instead, she forced herself to lean back into his embrace. As Doctor Nelson lifted a cold hand and cupped her breast through her lab coat, he shifted against her. Kali could feel his cock hard against her back, hinting at what the evening held in store. His eyes always held a fanatical glint, and over the last few weeks, it was getting worse.

"Yes, it is interesting. I look forward to working on him with you." She tried to force excitement into her voice, and it wasn't hard to summon it. However, it came from a source the doctor wouldn't have suspected. After months, she'd finally found the missing vampire. Now she had to play along with the doctor long enough to free him, so they could both escape.

"Don't get ahead of yourself. You still have to show me your appreciation for showing you the subject."

Kali fought the urge to gag at what he meant. His clumsy hands fumbled at the zipper of her pants, as he worked to strip them down. "Doctor Nelson, anyone could walk in—"

"I locked the door, and no one would think of disturbing me while I'm in my lab."

Unfortunately, Kali knew that to be true. No one in the lab seemed inclined to bother him anywhere unless they had to. Ever since she'd come to work for him six months ago, she'd seen firsthand how he treated his assistants, herself included. She wondered if she was the only one to receive his special brand of attention.

His hands slipped into her pants, and she summoned the last protest she could think of to buy herself some time. "It might wake up." She shuddered inside at her objectifying of the male vampire, but it was the only way she'd be able to stay close enough to do him any good.

"It's sedated. The only time we allow it to wake up is to watch it feed."

Kali gave up as her pants dropped to the floor, and her panties soon followed. Her skin crawled with each touch of the doctor's fingers upon her, but she gritted her teeth and allowed it. He seemed to take delight in humiliating her, and this was only the latest episode. Rather than move to the couch that rested along the wall, he bent her over the table the vampire was strapped to, and thrust hard against her. Biting her lip, her hands fisted together in the sheet next to the vampire's hand, she kept her stare locked on the almost angelic face of the vampire. He was her goal. As Doctor Nelson pounded into her, she forced herself to make the appropriate sounds of enjoyment, even as her mind raced with the implications of being shown the vampire.

The doctor thought she was as intensely passionate about his work as he was, trying to harness the key to eternal life. A true zealot. He'd dangled it in her face for months, until she finally gave in to his demands. Now he was making sure she paid for everything she received, but at the moment, it was a price she was willing to pay.

Tasting the metallic tang of her blood, she looked down and saw her blood dripping from her bit lip onto the vampire's face. Unable to take any more, she closed her eyes to ride out the last of the doctor's abuse of her body.

* * *

Several hours later, Kali sat down at her microscope, ignoring the twinges of pain that radiated through her body. After his climax, Doctor Nelson patted her ass and left her in the lab. As quickly as she could, she pulled her panties and pants up, shuddering at the feel of his sticky fluids seeping out of her. His callous disregard after sex was almost second nature by now. It had taken only a quick moment to slice a small cut into her arm and drain blood into the vampire's mouth. It wasn't enough to bring him to full strength, but she had to hope it would at least awaken him.

She waited for as long as she dared, but he never so much as twitched.

Sparing one last look at the vampire, she left the lab, more determined than ever to follow through with her plan. The vampire would be free, or she'd kill him herself. The doctor's plans for him would only get worse as his frustration grew.

From what she could see of Nelson's work, he'd taken a step back, rather than advanced, with his latest manipulations. He wasn't going to be happy when he figured it out. The cells she was observing were dying quicker since being introduced to his serum, rather than lasting longer as he had predicted.

'Why are you doing this?' The brush of the thought flitted against her consciousness. Pushing aside her own misgivings, she renewed her focus on what was contained on the slide.

'You need to get out while you can.'

Kali sighed and swept a wisp of ebony hair behind her ear. Leaning back in her chair, she tried to bring her thoughts into focus the way her martial arts instructor had shown her. Grand Master would have been appalled at how easily she doubted herself, and what she knew was right. Ever since she'd found out about the vampire's kidnapping, she'd known what she needed to do— free him at any cost. After everything she'd done to get this close, she couldn't turn back now. Her sacrifices wouldn't all be for nothing.

'He will kill you if he thinks you threaten his research. Leave now, and do not come back. I am not worth it.'

She jerked at the pronoun usage. 'I?' Opening her mind, she waited for a reaction, any reaction.

'Yes.'

Kali rubbed the bridge of her nose and resumed her focus on the microscope, maintaining the illusion in case the good doctor was watching her.

'*How?*' She asked, wondering if she was losing her mind. '*You were still under just a little while ago.*'

She felt a rush of rage, his rage, flowing over her as he answered. *It took a while to struggle past the lethargy of the drugs and lack of constant blood. I didn't have the ability to move.*

Kali swallowed heavily, licking at her sore lip. She remembered biting it so hard that she drew blood. '*You were awake*'? She asked, horrified he had witnessed her actions with the doctor.

'*Not at first. Your pain called me to consciousness, and then the scent of your blood started to overpower the effect of the drugs. The blood you fed me was enough to fully bring me awake, but it took time. They have not figured out yet that I am awake. They will be coming in soon to bathe me, and then I will take them down. Flee while you have the chance.*'

While the more cautious part of her wanted to urge him to wait until she could formulate a plan, she wasn't sure how much more of the doctor she could stomach. After months of being his plaything, forcing herself to pretend to enjoy his touch, she was tired of it. Now that the vampire was awake, it would make things much easier to get him out.

'If you can get out of the lab, you'll need help to get away. They've purposely kept you weak, just in case. What blood I could give you won't be enough.'

'It is too dangerous for you to be here. Go!'

Kali trembled at the mental push behind his words, but her Grand Master had prepared her for such an event. Focusing her thoughts, she pushed aside the compulsion.

'I'll be in the parking lot on the north side of the building. I'm driving a silver Mirage. I'll wait until you reach me, or I feel them kill you. Your choice.'

Calmly, as if she hadn't been having a mental conversation with a two-hundred-year-old vampire, she forced a yawn, then another. Rubbing the bridge of her nose again, she turned off her microscope, stored the slide, and headed out of the lab to her locker. Summoning another yawn, she moved down the hall to storage room. Acting as if it was just another end of shift, she stowed her lab coat.

Clipping her badge onto the collar of her shirt, she moved out of the room. Scanning the double doors at the end of the hall, she tried to send as much information as she could to the vampire. *'Can you see through my eyes?'*

'It would take a deeper connection. But I thank you. They are coming into the room. Leave now!'

Kali shivered at the force of his desperation. For some reason, her safety had become more important to him than his own. It went against everything Doctor Nelson had spouted, but fell in line with everything she knew about Grand Master. He might have been a vampire, but he'd been good to her after her husband's death. Without him, she would have ended her life long ago. It wouldn't take a psychiatrist to tell her that he was the driving force behind her risking her life to help a vampire she didn't know escape. She certainly knew it, just as she knew he had molded her to follow in his footsteps.

Walking calmly down the hall, she stopped at the guard station and waited her turn through the scanner. After they ascertained she wasn't carrying anything out, she moved to the employee's lounge where she grabbed her coat and purse. It took everything she had to stay calm, but she took the few moments required to casually chat with other employees gathering their things.

It would have seemed off if she hadn't, since much of the information she had gained on how to work Dr. Nelson had come from casual gossip. After faking another yawn, she was able to extract herself with the excuse she was exhausted. Given the long shifts many of them put in, it wasn't a stretch to understand.

Strolling to her car took the same great acting skills she used when pretending to enjoy the pawings of the maniacal toad she worked for. She had to pretend to be tired when all she wanted to do was break into a run and get to her car as quickly as she could. Putting her key into the driver's side door, she opened it and slid into the plush interior. Inhaling the soothing scent of lavender from her air freshener, she started the car, then purposefully spilled her purse on the floorboard. She caught glimpses of her coworkers getting into their own cars and driving away.

Leaning down, she slowly gathered her things, dropping them carelessly into the passenger seat.

'Come on, come on,' she whispered in her thoughts, not wanting to distract the vampire, but knowing he needed to hurry before he lost his chance. The guard on the next shift would pull in at any time, which would give the one at the desk backup. She knew they were poker buddies, and often spent half an hour or more at shift change chatting.

'I thought I told you to get out of here.'

Kali could feel his exhaustion with each word. He wasn't going to make it.

'Either you come to me, or I'll come and get you. Pick now'. As soon as she thought it, the door to the lab burst open and a naked man stumbled out. Slamming her car into reverse, she whipped out of her parking space and backed up to the door. Within a blink, the door was open and he jumped in. Jerking her gearshift to drive, she slammed her foot on the pedal and peeled out before he shut the door.

Ignoring the fact he was one hundred percent gorgeous, and that just having him in the car sent her hormone levels into overdrive, she concentrated on zipping down the road. She needed to leave the lab, and all the memories it contained, behind. Slamming a mental door shut before the events of the past few months could overwhelm her, she maneuvered the car into a parking garage and sped up to the third floor.

"What are you doing?" His voice sounded the same as it had in her head. Deep and velvety, with a hint of warmth—a dangerous combination.

"I have a car stashed here. You don't think I entered the lab under my real name, do you?" Pulling off the name badge, she opened the glove box and pulled out a plastic case. Unzipping it, she tossed the badge inside along with the contacts she peeled from her eyes, and every little scrap in the car.

Climbing out of the car, she reached under the back bumper of the car next to it, and pulled out a magnetic key box. Using the key it contained to open the door, she tossed everything from the Mirage into the new car--her own car.

After wiping down the steering wheel and door handles of the Mirage, she shifted her attention to the vampire lying almost comatose in the backseat.

"We need to get you out of here. Can you change cars without help?"

He nodded, his dark hair falling in wild disarray around his face. Her fingers itched with the urge to sweep it back. Damning the fragile connection her blood had forged between them, she moved to the trunk of her car and opened it, pulling out a duffle bag. Tossing it into the back seat, she waited while he collapsed into her car, then closed the door.

"We're almost home free," she reassured him, uncertain if he was even still awake.

They will not just let us walk away,' came the answer, whispering across her mind.

* * *

Kali checked her rearview mirror for what seemed like the hundredth time since leaving the lab, and breathed a sigh of relief that no one was there. It was almost daylight, and she was running on pure adrenaline. If she didn't pull over soon, she would end up falling asleep at the wheel, probably killing them both.

He'd stayed awake long enough to pull on the jeans and shirt she'd brought for him, then he nodded off. Soft snores drifted from the backseat for the past several hours. It was probably the first real sleep the vampire had enjoyed in a long while.

Spotting a hotel sign ahead, she pulled into the parking lot. Checking her purse for the ID she wanted, she turned off the car engine and headed inside. Within minutes, the sleepy-eyed clerk had taken her cash and assigned her a room. As luck would have it, it was on the corner, complete with easy access and outside of the view of the front desk. Knowing that didn't mean there were no cameras, so she was careful pulling into the space and moving her things inside. Returning to the car, she opened the back door and nudged the vampire awake.

His eyes flew open at the same moment he grabbed her neck, almost snapping it before the light of comprehension filled his gaze. As he let go, she collapsed against the seat, gasping softly for breath. Locking gazes with him, she tried to tamp down the fear that rose within her. She knew nothing about him, save that her Grand Master had believed him worth saving. If he hadn't died, it wouldn't have fallen to her to do the saving.

But he had, and she would carry out his last wish, even if the cost was her life. He'd saved her life once, the debt was owed. Regardless of what it took, she would pay it.

"We need to get you inside. It's almost light, and you're dangerously weak." The words sounded absurd as she said them. He could still easily kill her, even at partial strength. She knew too much time in the sun would sap what energy remained and he'd collapse. Without assistance and blood, the sun would drain his cells dry and he'd turn to ash.

Wrapping her arm under the dark-haired man's shoulder, she pulled him out, half holding him up as they struggled out of the car.

"Damn you're heavy," she grunted, dragging him into the room and to the bed, where he let go of her and flopped down, face first. Quickly moving to the door to close and lock it, she returned to his side.

"You're going to need blood," she stated. Biting her lip, she waited on him to respond. If need be, she could trick someone into returning to the room with her, and he could drink from them. She could offer herself, but he had to ask first.

"Yes." That was it, a simple agreement. Frustrated, she wanted to thump him for being so dense.

"Well? How do you want to do this? Do I get someone for you, or do you want me?"

He rolled onto his back, his eyes suddenly filled with heat. Kali swallowed as the double entendre of her words registered. "I mean, do you want my blood?" she backpedaled to clarify. Licking her lips, she waited for his answer.

"Your blood will strengthen our bond. We have already formed a mental connection. If I take more of your blood, I will be unable to control the need to claim you for my own, my body will demand it. You have already given your body for me, more times than I care to know of. I cannot ask it of you again. The choice, as they say, is in your hands."

Kali nodded and stalked off to the bathroom. *'I need to think,'* she conveyed in her mind, then closed a mental door. Almost immediately, she felt him pull back.

She smelled of Doctor Nelson's cologne and scent. Stripping off the offending clothes, she pulled the bag out of the trash can and tossed them into it. Once she turned the water on as hot as she could stand it, she stepped under the spray, needles of heat pounding against her skin. Her motions were jerky as she tried to block out the ramifications of her decision. She scrubbed at her skin until it was raw.

If she brought him someone, she'd feel guilty for the rest of her life. Innocence would be lost, and the karma would come back on her, she knew it. But the alternative, giving her body to a man--a vampire--she barely knew, seemed unimaginable. As the washcloth brushed over her pussy, she almost dropped to her knees from the sting of pain it evoked. Gasping, she grabbed the metal bar that ran the length of the tub and held on, white knuckled, until the pain ebbed. The sadistic bastard Nelson had hurt her before, but never this badly.

'What is wrong?'

Kali's head jerked up as his words flowed through her mind.

'Answer me, or I come in there.'

'The heat of the water surged. Someone must have flushed a toilet or something.'

'I will pretend that I believe you—for now.' Warmth swept over her, as he sent his concern for her through his thoughts before retreating once more, allowing her privacy.

Kali jerked her head in a nod before she remembered he couldn't see her. After she turned off the taps, she climbed out of the shower and toweled off. She wasn't certain when she'd made the decision, but she knew what she needed to do. Dropping the towel, she turned out the light and stepped out of the bathroom.

As she stepped around the corner, she registered that the overhead light was out, leaving only the dim glow of the nightstand lamp bathing the room. He had turned down the bed and was waiting, sitting on the edge.

"So you are going out to get someone—" His voice trailed off in a swift inhalation as she stepped further into the room.

Self-conscious, she ducked her chin against her chest, waiting for his reaction. It wasn't long in coming. Kali never heard him move, but suddenly he was standing before her, his fingertips gently lifting her chin. His ink-black eyes gazed down into hers, and Kali felt a curious stirring in the pit of her stomach. It was softer than the wave of lust that hit her in the car, but more poignant somehow.

"Are you sure?"

Tears filled her eyes at his soft tone. Blinking them away, she nodded and pulled her chin free. Moving around him, she grabbed the covers and pulled them to the foot of the bed before climbing in. Lying down, she tried not to look like a sacrificial virgin, but must have failed. He started to protest, but she swiftly cut him off.

"I made my choice. I can live with whatever happens between us, but I can't with taking the choice away from someone else."

"Someone else wouldn't compel me to lust at the first taste of their blood. I would be able to feed once from them. From you, I don't have that option. We are linked, and already my emotions for you are tangled up. The woman that you are draws me, and even as I know I should leave you be, I am compelled to claim you. To cherish your body, even as your blood nourishes me."

Kali nodded. Her gaze still locked on his, she lifted her hands to her hair and pulled it back, baring her neck. Arching against the pillows, she elongated the slender column as far as she could and waited while he seemed to struggle with himself.

As he moved to the bed, the wild thought that she didn't even know his name rushed over her. "If we're going to have sex, shouldn't I at least know your name?"

Warm lips brushed against her neck, sending tingles of awareness rushing over her. It felt right being here with him. So perfect.

"Riordan," he whispered against her skin, feathering soft kisses along the way. "My name is Riordan."

"I'm Kali," she whispered back, not trusting her own voice to a louder pitch.

"Sweet Kali, my savior, my angel, my greatest temptation." Reeling from his words, she didn't register the sting of his fangs as they sank in. Then she did, and the most intense pleasure followed. She felt like she was climaxing, the sensation spreading all over her body. She could hear the race of her heart, the thump-thump pounding in her veins.

'Shhhhh. I will take just enough to sustain me.'

She didn't doubt the sincerity of her words, not with the sudden strengthening of their bond. Through the link, she could feel how much it was troubling him to take from her, when she had already given so much. She could also feel the demand his body made, urging him to sink his cock into her while he fed, claiming her as his own. To strengthen the bond between them until nothing could separate them without their willing it.

Despite the events of the last few months, her own body made the same demand. It craved affection and pleasure after so much fear and pain. Every day she had dreaded waking up, knowing what she would have to suffer. Each morning walking into the lab, she had feared being found out for a fraud.

Her spirit demanded that she take something for herself, let Riordan sooth the ache that was building inside of her as his emotions blended with hers.

Parting her thighs, she slipped a hand between them, ignoring the sting of her pussy lips as she began to manipulate her clit. His fangs slipped free of her neck, and then his lips were against her breast. His teeth brushed against her nipple, teasing the peak into a tight bud before clasping it between them, slowly drawing it out. With soft kisses, he moved across her chest to her other breast, stroking his tongue softly over it in wet velvet flicks.

Kali arched against him, wanting to prolong the sensual torment.

He shifted lower, his lips blazing a trail of heat along her stomach. Pausing, he thrust his tongue into her belly button, swirling it around in the indentation, before dropping lower. Kali tried to push him away, to close her legs, but he grabbed her thighs and parted them, baring her swollen lips to his view.

"You hurt." Pain laced his words. She could feel his need to heal her, to make up for what was done to her.

"You don't have to--" she tried to protest.

"There is a healing agent in my saliva. It is what closes puncture marks. It will soothe your flesh." His lips pressed a soft kiss against her skin, then his tongue flicked out, lapping at her abused folds. Kali jerked at the flood of warmth that filled her.

'Relax.' His voice in her mind was soothing. His desire to ease her pain, to cherish her body flowed over her mind.

Fisting her hands in the sheet beneath her, she tried to push aside thoughts of how intimate what he was doing to her was, and to just feel. As his tongue thrust past her lips, stroking the inside of her pussy, she wanted to arch against him it felt so good. Of their own volition, her hips rocked forward, but the steel band of his arms wrapped around her legs, holding her still. All she could do was lay there and feel, while he stroked the heat of her need to a fever pitch.

Kali arched into his touch, her body on fire for more. She was like leaves on a forest floor, going up in flames at the slightest spark. She wasn't certain how he did it so quickly, but no sooner had his tongue left her body, than he was naked, his body pressed fully against her. As he settled into the valley of her thighs, she parted them, welcoming him. It felt right, almost as if he were fated to be there.

Clasping his shoulders, she curled her fingernails against his skin, leaving tiny crescent marks. A shudder rippled through him.

'*Again*', he whispered in her mind. Shifting her hands down, she raked her nails against his back, watching as he undulated against her. Without a doubt, it was the most seductive sensation in the world. She was so helpless against his strength, but with the merest of touches, she had him in the palm of her hand.

As she raked her nails down his back again, she was rewarded by a deep growl. His head lifted, and his gaze locked on hers. His eyes had gone molten.

"I do not wish to hurt you," he rasped, his voice tight with need.

In response, Kali wiggled beneath him until she could wrap her legs around his waist. Tightening them, she coaxed him to rest his cock against her entrance.

'Then don't leave me', she answered, trying to convey with her thoughts it wasn't just her body that would be left bereft. She had been so alone for so long, each day a struggle to find something to keep going for. Every since she had lost her Grand Master, she had been holding on to the need to fulfill his last request of her.

Now, in Riordan's arms, with her body coming alive as it hadn't in years, she wanted to live. What's more, she was coming to find as their bond grew, and their memories of their lives twined around each others, that he was very much a man she could come to love. She could feel his sinking deeper into her soul with every breath she took, until she was loosing the edge of where she ended and he began.

Riordan's lips slammed down against hers, bruising her mouth with his passion. Parting her own lips, Kali swept her tongue past to mate with his, claiming the role of aggressor for once in their mating. He held still, almost frozen above her.

Reaching between them, she wrapped her fingers around his cock and guided him past her pussy lips. As the first inch slipped in, she tried to relax. Her body was demanding more, but she knew if they rushed, pain would follow. Going slowly, she arched up against him, coaxing his cock in another inch.

Slickness increased as her body welcomed him. Tightening her legs, she rubbed her tongue against his as she sent one word through their mental link. '*More*'.

He responded with a passion that made her see stars. It was as if her demand had freed him from whatever held him immobile. One hard thrust, and they were fully joined. Kali gasped into his mouth as the bond began to exponentially increase in strength. She could hear her heart beating through his ears. If she closed her eyes, she knew she would see herself, lying there beneath him.

'*Mine*', he answered, an almost primitive instinct guiding him. She broke the kiss and burrowed her face into his neck, nodding against his sweat-slick skin. She could date for years and still never know all about a man that the last few minutes had stared about Riordan. Now she knew why Grand Master had always shied away from taking her blood. Even without the sexual component, the sheer emotional blending of the two would have been staggering to accept.

Riordan was only two hundred years old, but the joys and pain he had felt throughout his life was almost overwhelming. But even in the midst of the memory download that was occurring, she could only focus on the intensity of the here-and-now; the beat of Riordan's heart, the feel of his cock driving inside of her, the feel of his breath against her skin.

The bed creaked with the force of his thrusts as he started to move. Kali struggled at first to match the force of his rhythm, but soon fell in sync, her pussy contracting around his cock with each inward drive. Holding tight to his shoulders, she knew she drew blood but didn't care. The metallic scent of her own blood hung heavy in the air as she bit her lip again.

Riordan lifted his head from her neck and licked at her lips, rolling his tongue the tender skin before returning to her neck where he gently bit down.

Closing her eyes, she could almost see the threads that wound between them, merging them until they were no longer two separate entities. Grand Master had spoken of the bonding between a vampire and his mate, which was even more intense than a bond formed between two who cared for each other. His voice would fall soft in remembrance, but she never understood the true depth of his words until that moment. She felt whole in a way she hadn't before, even with her late husband.

Sparks began to ignite just under her skin, and the orgasmic euphoria of his drinking her blood resumed, building in intensity. Holding tight to his shoulders, she was afraid to let go for fear she would cease to exist. The pressure continued to build, each sensation rushing over her like a tidal wave. With a gasp, she realized his need fed her own, and hers was feeding his, until it was a continuous loop that built almost exponentially.

She wasn't sure how much more she could take, and then it crashed down over her. Screaming out his name, she orgasmed, her pussy tightening around him like a vise. She felt the answering flow of his passion into her, the warmth rushing up to her heart, then into her mind.

Trembling with the intensity of the doubled emotions, she wrapped her arms around his neck and held onto him, even when he would have moved to the side.

'I am crushing you.'

'No.'

Kali didn't expect it, but should have. In one smooth move, he rolled them over, so she lay spread out on top of him, her hair cascading around her face. Reaching up to push it aside, her fingers brushed against his. Tangling her fingers with his, she held on, the contact almost more intimate than their bodies still joined. Their hands rested against his heart, and she could feel the steady thump-thump against her knuckles.

Fear caused her heart to clench. He already meant so much to her. How would she bear losing him? "They'll come after you." She voiced her fear, needing to say it aloud.

Her body still sluggish with the aftermath of their passion, she kept her face pressed against his chest. The hand not holding hers lifted to her hair, smoothing out the tangled tresses. Moments of silence passed before Riordan spoke. "Yes, they will. But they only caught me the first time because I allowed it. We thought they would be less organized, and I would be able to break out. I was only planning to stay long enough to gather information, but they had a serum to put me to sleep. We weren't planning on that."

"We?"

Kali had through it was just her and her Grand Master. She didn't know of any others.

"My sire informed the council of elders, but they would not act without evidence for fear of what would happen if the rest of the human population found out about us. It angered him, but he understood why they were hesitant. Missing people and dead bodies eventually leave a trail. So he contacted me, and we went on from there, gathering what proof was needed."

"Mmm, I'd like to meet your sire." The idea of meeting an older vampire was daunting, but he was Riordan's family, of sorts.

"He would have loved you, I am sure. But he passed on a few months ago. He left behind a daughter, and asked me to take care of her should he die. Once I get the information to the council, I need to track her down and make sure she is safe."

Kali nodded her agreement against his chest, then shifted into a more comfortable position. Whatever the future held, they would face it together.

She felt confident her Grand Master would have approved of Riordan. It was strange, because ever since he adopted her, any man who came near her with even a hint of lust in his eyes was in danger of a beating.

Snuggling close against Riordan's warmth, she pushed worries about the future aside and simply reveled in the moment. It was something she hadn't been able to do in a long while.

She glanced at the clock beside the bed, noting sunrise was only minutes away. In case she woke early, she wanted to get a jumpstart on finding information for him.

"I'll start looking for your sire's child if I wake up first. We can go straight to the council and then move in to protect her."

Riordan nodded, his chin brushing against her head. "A good plan."

Kali smiled at his sleepy tone of voice. It'd been a rough few months for them both. She was already looking forward to the pull of sleep, but had to know the girl's name first.

"What's her name?"

'Calliope Martyn,' whispered through her mind.

Kali jerked upright, looking down at the vampire. "What? That's my name!"

A soft snore was the only answer she received. Looking out the window, she could see the faintest streak of daylight on the horizon. Riordan's features had softened in sleep, enhancing his natural beauty.

With a resigned sigh at her Grand Master's matchmaking, even from the grave, she gave up and laid her head on Riordan's chest. The need to sleep was too strong, and she no longer had the will to resist. But when he woke up, the vampire was going to get the surprise of his life.

* * *

Several days later, Kali snuggled against Riordan's chest, his strong arms wrapped around her, when the evening news cut to a breaking event. While she watched, the lab she had spent months working at was engulfed by flames. The anchorwoman related the sad news that premier Doctor Nelson apparently started the fire after the rest of his staff left for the evening. There was no hope of saving the doctor or the research conducted, especially given how secretive the doctor had been about what he worked on. Kali breathed a sign of relief—they were safe.

'The council started the fire?' She asked along their now constant mental bond.

She could hear the whisper of a sigh through his mind before he responded, *'Yes.'*

As she nodded, her head bumped against his chin, so she turned around to press a soft kiss against it. At that moment, Riordan dipped his head, and their lips pressed together.

'Calliope, my sweet Kali. My heart.' Passion ignited between them, racing back and forth, until they couldn't hold back any longer.

LAWS OF NATURE

Shay jerked against the handcuffs, glaring at the man who had slapped them around her slender wrists.

"This isn't funny, Bobby. Take off the damn cuffs before I kick your ass."

"Always so tough, Shaylee. You've just gotta prove you're one of the boys. Well you lied to me. You're not normal, and they're gonna make me big bucks to find out why not."

As he grabbed hold of her elbow and pulled her toward the car, she jerked against him. The realization that the cuffs were solid silver and the insane glint in his eyes drove home the fact Bobby wasn't joking. Spinning around on one leg as she kicked the other into the air, she slammed her foot against the side of his head. He bounced against the side of the car before crumpling to the ground.

Twisting her wrists in the cuffs only increased the sting of the silver. Biting back a curse of frustration, she looked around to make sure no one was watching, then tried to shift. As the familiar pain began to well within her, only to be tamped down by her reaction to the silver, she ground her teeth in frustration.

Forcing her pulse to calm, she began a light sprint down the street, her hands held awkwardly in front of her. With each step, the silver brushed against her skin, furthering the sting until a ring of red began to form where the cuffs rested against her wrists.

"Damn, Bobby," she growled while heading the last hundred yards to her house. Barely winded after almost a two-mile sprint, she opened the door and stumbled inside. Kicking it closed, she headed down the hall to her office, where she hoped to pick the lock. The only other alternative would be to call her family, and that would spell the end of her freedom. Although she knew she would have to call them anyway, if for no other reason than to warn them of the threat that rat-bastard ex-friend of hers posed, she didn't want to have one of her brothers ride to the rescue to undo the cuffs.

She had a paperclip unfolded and stuck in the lock, her teeth clamped on it, when a knock sounded against her front door. She froze, her heart pounding. She had forgotten to lock the door.

Stepping back into the room, her mind began running through her options. She was about to pick up the phone to call in the cavalry when the door swung open.

It took Shay a moment to register it wasn't Bobby in the doorway, but her neighbor Garrett.

"Shay?" Nervously he pushed his glasses up his nose and stepped toward her, his observant gaze not missing the handcuffs that shackled her wrists.

"Get out, and close the door behind you, Garrett."

"What happened, Shay?" As he spoke, he stepped into the room and closed the door behind him, flicking the lock.

"Bobby," she spat out, the word tasting foul on her mouth. Jerking in agitation, she hissed as the silver rubbed her already sore wrists.

Fire flared within Garrett's normally calm brown eyes. His boyish features tightened in anger, and for the first time in the two years she had known him, a curious awakening stirred within her. Gone was the boy next door, and in his place stood a man. As he stepped toward her and wrapped his hands around her wrists, a rush of desire moved through her.

"Let's get you out of these things." There was a gleam in his eyes she had often seen in her brother's gazes when they looked at women. He was pissed, and about to go alpha male on Bobby's ass. It only excited her further.

Swallowing the words that begged to be expelled, she cursed her hormones and the urge to mate that called. Garrett had always been safe— the sweet computer geek who lived next door. She should have known there was more to him.

Unable to speak, Shay nodded her consent, holding back the whimpers that formed as he twisted her wrists to get a better view. "Silver?"

"Yeah. I'm allergic to it."

"I remember."

Almost absently she nodded. Trust Garrett to remember everything, including the time he had purchased a silver necklace for her birthday and had to return it for a gold one.

As Garrett leaned down to grip the paperclip and begin working it in the lock, his hair brushed against her chin. Shay breathed in, the deep woodsy scent of his after shave swirled within her nose, further arousing her.

"I've almost got it, Shay. Just a second longer...there, got it." As the cuffs dropped free, his hands gently rubbed her wrists, soothing her abraded flesh.

"Thanks," she whispered, her throat tight. Her mind was still functioning, but her body was demanding control. The urge to jump him was building the longer she was near him.

"No problem, Shay. Now we need to call the cops and have him arrested. After I find him and beat the--" His words dropped off as he lifted his head, his gaze locking on hers. Looking into his deep brown eyes, Shay found herself drowning in need. Unable to resist, she tipped her head forward, brushing her lips over his.

With a soft groan, he pulled back. "Shay, what are you doing to me?"

His nostrils flared with each breath. She could see the desire in his eyes, the need to claim her slowly overwhelming him. It was matched by her own need to be taken, to have him claim her.

Forcing herself to step back, she tried to put some distance between them, only to have him move forward. Licking her lips, she stepped back again. Garrett followed, almost unconsciously.

"It's hormones, Garrett. You have to step back." She followed her own advice, only to have him counter it again.

"God, Shay, you're killing me. For two years I've lived next to you, watching you, dreaming of you. Needing you." Warmth bloomed within her at his words.

Stepping back, she bumped against the wall. As Garrett advanced, his thighs brushed against hers, then his groin pressed tightly into the cradle of her body.

Lifting her hands to his chest to push him away, she instead found herself caressing him through his shirt. Every breath he took ruffled her bangs, whispering over her skin.

"Why now?" he asked, wondering aloud.

"I'm in heat," she answered, unwilling to say so much, but needing to explain. At the same time, she worried he would have her committed. The old Garrett she knew wouldn't have, but he was something new. If the mating urge was as strong within him as it was rushing through her, she knew he wouldn't be able to let her go. But she couldn't help wondering if Garrett could accept what she was.

"Heat?"

"Garrett," she whimpered as his hips ground against her. "I can't think."

"Good," he responded, his lips brushing over hers. "Too much thinking for too long."

Indulging in the feel of his mouth pressing against hers, Shay parted her lips. His tongue immediately took possession of her mouth, thrusting deep to rub against her own. A breathless growl welled in her throat.

Her hands fisted in the Egyptian cotton of his shirt, holding him tight against her as she allowed him to claim her mouth. Sparks of desire burst within her pussy, and she could smell her own need. Before the world could fall away, she broke the kiss.

"I'm not human," she gasped out, the need to mate riding her hard.

Some of the glazed look left his eyes as he tipped his head back, questions flashing through his eyes. Confusion softened his features, making him appear more like the Garrett she was used to.

"It's why Bobby cuffed me; he was going to turn me in somewhere where they would run experiments on me."

As soon as she said it, she wished she could call back the words. His face tightened, anger flashing in his eyes. "I'm a *were*, Garrett. My whole family is, except for two of my sisters-in-law."

"*Were?*"

Rather than the disbelief she'd expected, he seemed to believe her. "I'm a shape-shifter." In other circumstances, it would have sent her into peels of laughter; here she was pressed from breast to hip against the man she now knew to be her life-mate, with the need high upon her, and rather than fucking like werebunnies, they were having a serious conversation.

Although, if he shifted his hips one more time, that would end, because her brain would short circuit.

"Maybe we should sit down and talk," she offered. He growled in answer, and pressed closer. "Okay, then."

"You change into what exactly?"

"It depends. Look, Garrett, do you want the twenty second version or the whole long story, which could take hours?"

He rocked his hips against hers in response. As a flash of heat rushed over her, causing her to gasp and grind against him, she tried to form a coherent thought.

"There's a gene that runs in my family which allows us to shift. Because of breeding between the lines, there are no longer werewolves, werecats, and so on. We are all just *were*. When we reach puberty, the urge will begin to run us, and we'll have to shift. We never know what we'll become, unless we take matters into our own hands."

She tightened her grip on his shirt as he dipped his head, pressing soft kisses along her neck. Even though she was glad he wouldn't have her committed, she wasn't so happy he was trying to drive her insane.

"Go on."

"Because the line isn't pure, introducing the genetics of another animal into our own before the first change denotes that as our creature. Many of our kind visit the zoo at night during our teens, and select an animal. We either have to get them to bite us, or we draw their blood and inject it into our veins."

His hands cupped her ass, lifting her against him. Back against the wall, Shay wrapped her legs around his waist.

"Garrett," she moaned, her hands slipping down between them to undo the buckle of his belt.

"What did you choose?"

Shay laughed self-consciously. "I wanted to be a leopard. But when I got to the zoo, I heard another creature crying in pain. When I tried to help it, it bit me. I finally got it calmed down, and helped it as best I could. But the damage was done."

He rocked against her, his cock pressing tight against the layers of clothes between them. Shay whimpered as she arched, pressing the hard beads of her nipples against his chest.

"What do you become?"

Shay tucked her head into the curve of his shoulder, nipping at the column of his neck.

"Tell me," he demanded, his hands tightening on her ass.

"A fox, okay? I wanted to be something big when I shifted, something badass, since I couldn't be in human form. But I got bit by a damn endangered bat-eared fox."

"Show me." At first she thought he had to be kidding, until he untangled her legs from around her waist. As he stepped back, she got a good look at him. Normally immaculately groomed, his brown locks were ruffled, some standing on end. His glasses sat crocked on his nose, and his pants were half unzipped, the belt lying undone.

He had never looked better to her.

He lifted a hand to her face, cupping her cheek in his palm. "I need to know we're not both crazy; me for believing you and you for thinking you can shift. Show me," he half begged, half demanded.

Moving around him, Shay grabbed the edge of her T-shirt and pulled it over her head. Garrett groaned as his gaze moved over her body, blazing a trail of heat in its path. With her hands at her waist, she unzipped her jeans and slid them down her hips. As she stood there before him, his gaze almost worshipful as it moved over her, she had never been happier with her lithe, petite frame.

Barely five feet tall, she'd always cursed her height, but standing against his slender frame, she found it was a perfect match.

"Are you ready?" she asked, almost afraid of his answer. Garrett took a deep breath and nodded, his Adam's apple bobbing as he swallowed heavily.

Closing her eyes, Shay called the change to come forth, and as the pain prickled her skin, she dropped to her knees. She could feel her skull shifting, her bones morphing. Hair rippled over her skin, covering her in a layer of soft gray fur.

A breath later, she opened her eyes and stared up at him. A look of wonder had covered his features; his eyes alight with the knowledge that more things existed than he had previously known. She had seen it on the face of one of her two mortal sisters-in-law when she had watched her brother change.

"Shay?" Uncertainty laced his words as he dropped to his knees before her, his hand caressing her soft fur. Licking his palm, she pressed her face against the soft skin and yipped. He leaned forward and pulled her silk panties and bra from around her form where they had gotten tangled during the change. As he rocked back, she moved away.

"Changing back?"

Yipping softly, she closed her eyes and called the change again. Easier to return to normal than to shift to animal, she was able to stand as soon as the change was done. Opening her eyes, she caught the disorienting glimpse of movement as Garrett stood and picked her up, his hands cupping her ass and holding her tight against him. His lips locked on hers, with his tongue sweeping between them, as he headed down the hallway to her bedroom.

Shay wrapped her arms around his neck and locked her ankles together behind his back. As he moved to the bed, she bit his earlobe. "The wall," she gasped out, almost unable to think with the pulsating need coursing through her body. She just knew she couldn't wait, and the bed meant more foreplay and slow lovemaking. She wanted it hot, fast and *now*!

Garrett pressed her against the wall, his hips grinding the soft denim of his jeans against her pussy. Gasping softly, she reached between them to finish unzipping his pants. Her hands encountered bare skin. Wiggling to get his pants around his hips, she brushed against the head of his cock.

"Going commando?" she asked into his mouth, then giggled softly. With a jerk, he sent his pants to the floor and stepped out of them.

It took both of them, and a lot of fumbling, but they finally got his shirt off and then blessedly bare skin pressed against bare skin.

Holding onto his shoulders, Shay lifted up and pressed down against his cock, slipping the first inch into her welcoming warmth. She bit her lip at the delicious rush of sensations.

Dipping her head into the curve of his neck, she pressed soft kisses along his shoulder as he thrust up against her, driving himself further into her pussy. Clenching her muscles tight, Shay almost screamed with the need for him to hurry, but he set a leisurely pace, his hips barely rocking against hers.

After the intense foreplay in the hallway, she was almost ready to scream in frustration.

"Fuck me, Garrett," she growled, grinding down against him. Sliding her hands down his shoulders, she gripped his upper arms and leaned back, almost sitting upright as she braced herself between the wall and him.

His eyes closed and his head tipped back. Shay nipped at the base of his throat, licking away the sting as Garrett picked up the pace, driving hard and fast into her. Holding on tight with her legs and hands, Shay relaxed into the pounding, her body demanding more.

Almost delirious with need, she started whispering dirty words against his skin as she nipped her way along his chest. Her pussy clenched with each thrust, until they fell into a steady rhythm that pushed her higher and higher.

Undulating against him, Shay worked to drive them both into orgasm together. She could fell the tightness expanding within her, the rush of her blood through her veins heralding the climax to come. As it built, she clenched her pussy as tight as she could, milking his cock.

As her orgasm claimed her, pounding at every fiber of her body, she screamed his name, her nails digging into the skin of his forearms.

An answering groan followed, as warm jets of his cum filled her. Inhaling deeply, she could smell the mixture of their scents, which sent her spinning off again. Darkness rushed over her, and she blacked out.

When she came to, she found herself lying on her bed, Garrett leaning over her, concern darkening his brown eyes to black.

"You okay?"

Shay nodded and reached for him, pulling him down for a kiss. "Now I am."

Although the edge had been taken off, she could still feel the desire for him sleeping beneath the surface, ready to awaken at any moment. From what her mother had told her, it would always feel that way, now that she had found her mate.

Her mate. As the thought rushed over her, a warmth settled against her heart. Garrett, her sweet friend who always had time on Friday nights when she wanted to curl up and watch a movie, and when she cried about her sucky boyfriends. The same Garrett she'd always feared was gay, especially with how often one particular guy kept coming over.

Unable to help herself, she blurted out happily, "You're not gay."

Warm laughter rushed over her as Garrett leaned down and nuzzled the underside of her breasts. "Nope."

"But what about your visitor?"

"Stephan? He's my kid brother, and yes, he is very much into guys."

As a new worry came to her, Shay sighed. Garrett's head popped up, and he arched a brow at her. She didn't know how she had ever seen him as boyish, since everything about him screamed territorial male. Which was part of the reason why she was hesitant to broach the subject she knew she had to—her ex-friend.

"Bobby is still out there. I don't know how much he knows about my family, but considering that he knows about me, I fear they'll be his next targets."

Tension radiated from him as he slowly moved back and climbed from the bed. "Did you tell him?"

As much as he tried to be nonchalant, Shay could tell her answer mattered a lot to him. "No. You're the first person I've told. We are only allowed to tell—"

She slammed her lips shut as she realized what she was about to reveal. It was too soon, but as he turned back toward her, with his head cocked to the side, she could tell he was already considering the possibilities.

"Only allowed to tell who?"

Shay swallowed and sat up, her body still lethargic with the aftermath of two orgasms. "Our mates."

"Then how does he know?

"That I don't know, but it's just one of the things I need to find out. And soon."

* * *

There was no doubt about it, Garrett was pissed, and getting more so by the minute. As soon as she'd admitted she didn't know how Bobby knew about her, it jolted him into action. He quickly gathered their clothes, and amid quick kisses, they'd gotten dressed and out the door.

The couple of miles between her house and Bobby's seemed to pass in slow motion for Shay. It seemed she had run the distance quicker than they were now driving it.

As they pulled into the driveway, blocking Bobby's car, she watched every muscle in Garrett's body tense. He took several deep breaths, his nostrils flaring with each one.

"If he doesn't give us answers—" Shay turned toward him and pressed her fingers against his lips. She knew he wanted to rip Bobby's head off—so did she. But she had to know the extent the threat against her.

Not wanting to give Bobby a chance to make a run for it, she pushed open her door and climbed out. Closing it as quickly and quietly as she could, she stalked to the house, Garrett close on her heels.

Hoping he hadn't changed the locks, Shay found the key to Bobby's house and put it into the lock. As the door swung open, she flashed Garrett a quick smile. Stepping into the house, she cocked an eyebrow at Bobby who stood waiting with a taser aimed at her. As Garrett stepped into the house behind her, Bobby turned white and stepped back.

"Happy to see me, I take it," Shay said dryly.

His hand started to tremble, but he kept the taser pointed at her chest.

"You shouldn't have run, Shay. Now I gotta get mean, and I don't like that."

"Shove it, Bobby," she responded. "You pissed off the wrong woman." Bobby's eyes widened as Garrett pulled a small pistol out and aimed it at him.

"Now drop the taser and sit the hell down."

As he moved to obey, the whites of his eyes clearly visible, she turned and ran a hand through her hair. Wanting to kick him for bringing her to this point, she cursed under her breath and tried to calm down.

Garrett wasn't having as much trouble. From the sounds behind her, Bobby wasn't moving fast enough for his liking. The sound of a fist striking flesh had her turning to see Garrett knock down the taller man.

"I'd stay down if I were you," she advised as she crouched in front of him.

"Who hired you to kidnap me?"

Bobby pursed his lips, the stubborn glint in his eyes very familiar to her. "Look, Bobby, we were friends, at least I thought we were. So out of the spirit of that friendship, I'm going to give you some advice. Unless you want to get the crap kicked out of you, I would answer the questions."

Chickenshit that he was, Bobby nodded and spilled what he knew. Thirty minutes later, a knock sounded against the door and Shay moved to open it, while Garrett stood against the wall, his ankles crossed and trying to look nonchalant while still aiming the gun at Bobby. His eyes betrayed him. Despite his relaxed demeanor, she could tell he was just waiting for Bobby to move so he could pummel the man who cuffed her into ground beef.

Opening the door to admit two of her brothers, Shay quickly filled them in on the details she'd been able to piece together.

"So basically, there's a scientist who's trying to find the fountain of youth, and is willing to pay top dollar for non-mortals. Somehow, he found out about us, and after digging up some dirt found out that Bobby had some serious gambling debts. And some very pissed off people wanting to collect."

"Why you, though?" Shay turned at her brother's comment and punched Ruben in the arm. "Evidently being the pipsqueak you always called me, I was deemed the easiest target. Using Bobby also gave them an advantage with me. But they might still come after you guys, or anyone else in the family."

Turning to look at her other brother, Shay could see the gears turning behind his dark eyes. He was holding on by a thin thread, and any moment he could snap. Speaking to him was like holding nitro, she had to watch every movement.

"What are you thinking, Vance?"

He turned his gaze toward her, and for a moment, she saw the depth of his love for her until blind rage removed it. "I think I'm going to turn *your friend*," he sneered, "over to the folks and then I'm going after this scientist, Dr. Nelson. And when I'm done with him, baby sister, I had better find you wearing an engagement ring or I will go after the man in the other room."

Unfortunately, Garrett chose that moment to walk into the room, leading a reluctant hostage. "Sorry to bust up your planning party, folks, but you need to turn on the news."

Shay quickly crossed the room to the TV and flipped it on. Surfing the channels, she soon found a news station, which was covering a lab fire that had just broken out.

"That's it," Garrett stated.

Bobby gasped as the camera zoomed in on the building, dropped to his knees then started crying. Uncertain why, Shay focused on the TV, until the anchorwoman calmly informed the viewers that the head of the lab, a scientist named Nelson had perished in the fire.

"Son of a bitch!" Vance exclaimed, frustration radiating in his words.

"What?" Shay couldn't help the feeling of relief that swept over her, even as she felt guilty for it—a man had died, after all.

Vance's brows furrowed in anger. "All his research is gone. His notes, everything. How the hell are we supposed to discover how he found out about us, who else knows, and how big the threat is?"

The enormity of his statement hit Shay like a punch to the chest. Looking at Garrett, she could see it having much the same effect. All her life she had known she had to guard her secret, that only when she mated would she be able to reveal her true self.

But now, someone else might know. Someone who would be coming after her.

"You get home, baby sister. Lock the doors and stay holed up until we get back. We're going to take Bobby here to the folks and let them decide what to do with him, and then we'll be back as soon as we can. Pack what you need, and we'll replace the rest."

"No."

Three incredulous faces turned toward her. Bobby was too busy sobbing about how the loan shark was going to come after him to pay them much attention.

"I am not going to go into hiding. I will go home, but not to pack up and leave."

"Shay--" Ruben began, always the voice of reason.

"No!"

Only Garrett remained silent, his brown gaze steady on her face. Half nodding, he winked at her.

"Shay has a point, guys. She doesn't know who she's hiding from, or even if there is a continued threat. Nelson might have been alone in this, for all we know."

Vance growled at the younger man, fur rippling down his arm before he could get himself under control. "You willing to risk my sister's life on that belief?"

"No. But I am willing to stand behind my mate and her decisions. She's not a coward, and neither am I."

Shay gasped as Garret spoke. It was the first time he had accepted verbally what she had called him. She wasn't certain exactly when he came to terms with it, but if she had to guess, it must have been the moment after he said it, judging by the stunned look on his face.

Both brothers tried to stare him down, and the minutes passed in tense silence, broken only by an occasional sob from the man lying on the floor.

Reluctantly, Ruben nodded and looked away. Shay held her breath as she waited for the alpha of her brothers to make his decision. His eyes flickered, then his gaze finally dropped, causing her to feel a rush of dizzying happiness.

Garrett couldn't know it, but Vance had just acceded to Garrett's mate claim, leaving her well-being in his hands. They trusted him with not just her life, but with her health and happiness, too.

Turning away, her oldest brother leaned down and grabbed Bobby by the underarms and lifted.

Ruben stepped in and grabbed his ankles, and they started toward the door.

Shay moved to stand beside Garrett, her hand reaching for his while she watched her brothers leave. Neither paused, or turned back.

As Ruben pulled the door closed behind them, she sighed in relief. She turned to face the man who was quickly becoming her whole life.

"I know you thought you were just backing me up, but, Garrett, what you said…" She paused, uncertain how to tell him the meaning her family would find behind his words.

He lifted the hand not holding hers and cupped her cheek. As his thumb stroked over her skin, she fought the urge to purr, it felt so good. The need to mate with him was awakening within her.

"I know what I said is not something to be taken lightly." He dipped his head and placed an all-too-brief kiss against her lips. Shay pulled her hand away and grabbed fistfuls of his shirt with both hands, clinging to him when he pulled back. "I've waited two years for you to notice me. In that time, I've gone from lusting after you to loving you."

"Garrett," she whispered, her chest tight.

"I'm just so worried someone will come after you, and I'll lose you; either to your brothers' protection or to someone trying to experiment on you."

"I love you too," she responded, needing to say the words, and knowing instinctively he needed to hear them. "And that's what matters. As for the rest, we will figure out what happened, not just how the doctor found out about me but also what caused the fire that killed him."

Pressing a soft kiss against his cheek, Shay shifted to nip at his earlobe. "But for now, let's go home, where you can make love to me in a bed this time."

Garrett groaned like a starving man offered a feast and picked her up in his arms, cradling her against his chest. "We have to go shopping first. I need to get a ring on your finger before your brother comes back and kills me."

Shay sucked on his earlobe as he carried her to his car, and deposited her gently into the passenger seat.

He quickly closed the door and moved around to the driver's side and slid in. Once he started the engine, Shay leaned back in her seat while he backed the car up and shifted into drive, then started down the road.

Lids half closed, Shay watched his reaction as she unzipped her pants. She loved the way his eyes widened as she slipped a hand into her panties and started caressing her pussy.

"Shaylee, are you trying to get us killed?"

"Since you're so determined to go shopping, I need to take the edge off."

Garrett groaned again, the sounds coming out strangled. The car picked up speed, and they fairly flew the few miles home. By the time he pulled into the driveway, Shay was about insane with the need to feel him deep inside her. She'd been holding off her orgasm for the last half-mile, waiting until they got home.

"I take it we're going shopping later?"

Garrett didn't respond. He didn't need to.

Shay pulled her hand out of her pants and threw the door open before the car fully stopped. Laughing over her shoulder, she raced up the walkway to her house and unlocked the door, Garrett fast on her heels.

BOUND IN BLOOD

Anya tried to hide her surprise while the council members yelled at each other. Ever since the call had come in about a threat to their people, the council had been trying to decide what to do about it. As the normally quiet Lady Kathlyn slammed her fist down on the table and bared her fangs at the unofficial spokesperson for the council, Anya winced. Things were going to flame out of control, and very quickly, if someone didn't step up to calm everyone else.

"We have to destroy the lab and everything in it. We can't take the risk—" Kathlyn was cut off as another council member kicked his chair back into the wall and stalked to the other side of the room. His hands fisted at his side, revealing his fury.

"What about the others? Do we let the shifters know about the threat?" Another of the councilors spoke up, then sat back down as several others glared at him. Anya held back the urge to hiss at him in rage. It was one of their own who had been taken, it was the vampires' place to take care of the situation.

"While we're sitting here bickering, there's no telling what this Dr. Nelson is planning. He must be stopped!" Lady Kathlyn continued to push her point home, and judging from the nodding heads of those still sitting, she was swaying them. "Riordan suffered so much at his hands, and his chosen was willing to give up her life to save him.

We cannot let their suffering be for nothing. We have to *stop* this evil maniac!"

With a deep sigh, the head of the council nodded and raised a hand in a call for quiet. "While I don't like it, the only option we have managed to come up with is to kill the ringleader of this nightmare and destroy his research. In spite of Lady Kathlyn's opinion, we need to call a gathering of all the elders and inform not only the other sects of our kind but also the shifters. We all have to be aware of the threat and prepared for any possibility."

* * *

Anya grumbled silently as she settled in for another long night. Taking care of Dr. Nelson and setting the fire in the lab had been fairly easy, given the information Kali and Riordan had been able to provide. It had gotten a little dicey when the cops, firemen and news crews arrived and wandered all over the place. But she had faded into the shadows and held herself motionless for the several hours it took for the firefighters to finally douse the fire.

Now, she was still waiting. She wasn't sure for what, but the back of her neck had been tingling for a while and she trusted her instincts too much to ignore it. The council had entrusted her with many vital missions over the years, but never one as important as this. None of the research done at the lab could be allowed to continue, and that meant she had to be certain everything was destroyed, and everyone involved in it.

A faint rustle sounded off to her left, sending her already screaming nerves into overdrive. Inhaling, she could smell the faint tang of sweat on the night breeze. Mixed with the scent was another she was well familiar with – the metallic sweetness of blood.

Inhaling again, she detected an undercurrent to the blood that teased her senses as she tried to identify it. As the unknown male moved closer, she forced herself to remain motionless until he was within reach. Striking fast and deadly, she had her knife out and pressed against his throat before he ever had a chance to react.

"Move and you're dead."

The male remained completely still, his body pressed tightly against hers. Shifting closer, she used her free hand to search him for weapons even as her senses were scanning for anyone with him.

As she reached into the cuff of his boots, while still holding the blade against his throat, Anya felt a bolt of sensation slamming through her. Cursing her body's reaction to the teasing hint of blood and prime, hormone pumping male, she mentally detached herself and continued with her job.

After assuring herself he wasn't carrying any weapons, she stood up again and pressed tight against him, her voice a whisper in his ear. "We're going to sit down, and you're going to tell me who you are and what you are doing here, or else we're going to have a big problem. Now, nice and easy, drop to your knees."

The feel of the male sliding down her body, brushing against her breasts and groin on the way down stirred the need that was demanding attention.

Once he had settled on the ground, she carefully moved around in front of him, her eyes widening slightly as she got a good look at him. The strange scent to his blood made perfect sense when she glimpsed the tattoo that adorned his upper arm. It clearly marked his family line and inner beast. Clad in a black sleeveless T-shirt and jeans, the corded muscles of his arms flexed slightly as he returned her gaze.

"What are you doing here, Shifter?"

His dark eyes slowly met hers, the pupils elongating until they were more cat than human. "I'm here for answers." Anger laced his words as he fairly spit them out. Fur started to ripple along his arm, slashes of orange and black, then fading back to deeply sun-kissed skin.

Anya swallowed at the bolt of lust that almost knocked her off her feet. She wanted to feed from him, to lie trapped beneath his form as he offered her his throat. Unfortunately, until she was certain he wasn't part of the problem she had come to take care of, she didn't dare indulge in such fantasies.

But judging by the flaring of his nose as he inhaled sharply, he had caught the brief moment of desire she had allowed herself, and knew her body was wet and tight with need.

"I might have something to offer. But first, who are you?"

His eyes locked on hers, he offered a facsimile of a smile. It reminded her of a wolf she had once seen, baring its teeth moments before it struck.

"Name's Ruben, and as you already guessed I'm a shifter. Now yours, Vamp."

"What are you doing here?"

Vance shook his head, sending the waves of his hair ruffling in the breeze. She could smell the briefest hint of his shampoo and knew with his enhanced smell he could probably tell a lot more about her than she wanted him to. "Quid pro quo, Clarice. You get nothing more from me until I get something from you."

Her lips quirked as the reference to one of her favorite scenes between Hannibal Lector and Clarice in 'Silence of the Lambs'. It was rare to find anyone who appreciated the finer points of the movie enough to memorize lines.

"I'm Anya. And yes, I am a vampire."

Ruben shifted, rocking back and settling his firm ass on the ground.

"The scientist who worked here, he tried to have my sister kidnapped," He offered.

Anya's mind started whirling at the implications. Someone else knew of the doctor's research. But who? "Do you know who it was? Do you have the person contained? How many more are involved?"

"You're breaking the rules again, Anya."

"Damnit, this isn't a game," she snapped, ready to knock him out and present him to the council for questioning if she didn't start getting answers.

"No, this isn't a game. But quite frankly, you don't know me, I don't know you, and we would both be fools to just offer up what we know."

Anya nodded and slowly shifted her position so that she could kneel on the ground near him. Holding her dagger in her hand, she settled herself. "One of our kind was captured and tortured. We got him back."

"The man who tried to kidnap my sister has been taken care of."

Anya trembled at the finality in his tone. Shifters could be fiercely protective, especially of their females. It wasn't unheard of for male shifters to shred someone who threatened a female. As much as some of the elite liked to think the races differed, vampires could be just as animalistic in their efforts to protect their children and the weakest of their kind.

Clenching her fist around the dagger hilt at the memory of how quickly and peacefully she had dispatched the doctor, she focused on the here-

and-now. She hadn't had time to make him pay for what he had done to both Riordan and Kali, and she had wanted to. Very badly.

"We don't know if anyone else is involved. We have a source that believes he was too egotistical and greedy to involve anyone else at any real level in his research. But there are those who know, those who captured his specimens."

Ruben's eyes went more animal at her words. A faint growl rumbled up from his chest, startling all the animals nearby into silence. Moments passed in silence until he spoke again. "We need to pool our information."

Anya nodded. The council had planned to do just that, and for all she knew, they already had while she stood watch. "Agreed."

She wasn't expecting him to move, so the suddenness of it caught her off guard. She found herself flat on her back, trapped beneath his form before she had chance to struggle. Her fangs ripped through her gums and she started to bring up the dagger before the nature of his move registered.

He was nuzzling at her neck, inhaling deeply. His body was completely relaxed over hers, his arms braced to hold most of his weight off her more slender body.

"Get off of me, Cat," she snapped as the need to feed surged. She could hear the blood racing through his veins, calling to her like the strongest of aphrodisiacs. It didn't help that he smelled so damn good, and the feel of him covering her sent her body to craving more skin-to-skin contact.

Rather than roll off her, he pulled back, his groin pressed tightly into the V of her thighs and lifted a hand to her face. Lightly rubbing his thumb over her lips, he pressed the tip past them to stroke over one of her fangs.

She instinctively swallowed as drops of blood trickled down her throat. Looking into his eyes, she could see the same intense need that was coursing through her—he wanted to sink into her body.

"Now isn't the time, but we're not done yet." Her pussy clenched at the sensual promise in his voice. Sucking his thumb into her mouth, Anya rolled her tongue over the puncture, healing the wound. Then before he could guess her intent, she flipped him off her and kicked her feet as she arched up, propelling herself into a crouch, then stood.

* * *

Several hours later, she was ready to crawl out of her skin. Ruben's family elders had arrived, as had his sister and brother, his sister's mate, and as many local vampires as could make it such short notice. The council chambers had been turned into a meeting hall, packed with shifters and vampires. Emotions were running high, fear thickened the air, and it was all she could do to breath slowly and evenly as people shifted, bumping into her.

Nerves already shot, she wasn't sure how much more she could take. To make matters worse, the sun was about to come up and she had yet to feed or to cash in on Ruben's offer. Although she could go without feeding until the next evening, her body's need wasn't going to be so easy to ignore. He had started an itch and her flesh was creaming for him to scratch it.

"Until we know for certain that the threat is at an end, we need to take precautions." Anya found herself agreeing with Ruben's brother. Although it bothered her that he had been the one to broach the subject, and knew that some of the other vampires were feeling less happy as the rumbling of the voices in the room increased.

Unlike the others though, she had seen the lab and its equipment firsthand. She had no desire to wind up there as a lab rat. That gave her a head-start on the others.

Unconsciously, her gaze shifted to the vampire who had been held captive there. He'd suffered so much and yet, never broke. Already, there were rumblings that Riordan would be nominated to the council when a seat became open.

A soft growl sounded softly in her ear as Ruben shifted closer, pressing tight against her side. It only served to frustrate her more. He had no business going territorial on her. She wasn't his mate, and her long-term plans didn't leave much room for a male—any male—let alone a shifter who was hell-bent on protecting her.

It was her job to protect others, not be the protected.

"To that end, the council and the elders have agreed we need to work together." The volume in the room dropped off as soon as Lady Kathlyn spoke. "We're vulnerable during the day. That's how they managed to capture Riordan, and it took a day-walker to free him." It was almost deathly silent before she was done. "So all unattached vampires will be partnered in groups or singly with shifters, depending on what tasks they perform."

At the lady's words, Anya jerked. Ruben chose that moment to slide his hand down her back, stopping just above the waist of her leather pants, where he started to trace small circles on her skin with his thumb.

"The vampires will also protect the shifters, as at night they are stronger and more dangerous than anything that could be thrown at us." Ruben growled his agreement to his brother's words, as did many of the shifters in the room. Unlike her people, shifters were tactical masters and weren't above using any advantage to protect their people.

"I'll be expecting total cooperation in this." Lady Kathlyn's steely tone made it clear that she expected complete obedience to the council's wishes, as was her right.

As much as Anya wanted to protest, the council had spoken.

The pairing off of the groups only took a few minutes and ended as she had expected—Anya has been ordered to stick with Ruben. His sister Shaylee and her mate were partnered with Riordan and his wife, and were requested to stay near the council for the near future, which made sense—they might still have valuable information to contribute.

What was unexpected was that Ruben's older brother, the next alpha of his family, was going to be Lady Kathlyn's only shadow. Normally at least two vampires, generally slightly older protectors who were still in their prime but seasoned by field work, guarded the council members. For only one shifter to be assigned to her was odd, but it wasn't Anya's place to question.

The rest of her people were assigned shifters according to compatible jobs. Although she hadn't met any of the other shifters, she had a feeling she was going to come to know some of them very well in the coming weeks.

As everyone filed out of the room, Lady Kathlyn called for Anya to stay behind. The other council members left as well, leaving just the two vampires and Ruben in the room.

"Anya, I know this must be hard for you, but we need you to help set an example. If the council and its protectors are willing to accept help, then it is hoped it will make it easier for weaker vampires to do so as well."

"Yes m'lady." There wasn't much else to say. As much as she hated to admit it, there was a lot of validity to the lady's point. Those who were stronger had to make the point that it wasn't weak to accept help. She wondered if it was the same for the shifters, and if that was why Ruben's brother had been partnered with the youngest and most outspoken of the council members.

For a brief moment, a hint of uncertainty passed over the lady's face before her features settled back into their normal tranquil expression.

"If that's all?" Anya asked.

At the councilor's nod Anya turned on her heel and left, Ruben quickly falling into step beside her.

"What's a protector?" Ruben's words pulled her out of her contemplations, making her away of the lethargic state of her limbs.

"Me," she snapped, the growing brightness of the horizon calling her to sleep. She quickened her pace as much as she could, but still barely made it to her quarters and inside the lightless room before dropping to her knees. As young as she was, she hadn't built up as much of a resistance to the sun's call as those older vampires. Sometimes the council members forgot that fact when they called her to audience with them. Luckily, protectors were all given rooms in the council's mansion.

Ruben crouched beside her and lifted her into his arms. "Make yourself at home," she slurred before unconsciousness claimed her.

* * *

When Anya woke the room was dark and her mouth felt stuffed with cotton. She tried to lift her hand to rub her face, but found it restrained. The feel of the sheets against her skin gave away her lack of clothing. For a brief moment she felt a spurt of panic—the doctor hadn't been working alone and they had found her people.

Then a familiar scent teased her nose. Ruben.

A match struck, then a flare of light as he lit one of her candles. Sandalwood.

"Why am I tied down?" she growled. Licking at her dry lips, she winced at the pain in her gums. It matched the hollow feeling in her stomach. She needed to feed, and soon.

Rather than answer, Ruben lit another candle. The scent of musk filled the air, blending with the sandalwood. The flickers of light the candles produced were enough for her to see the play of Ruben's muscles as he moved along the side of her bed. He was naked, and very aroused.

"Did you know that you cry out in your sleep?"

Anya shook her head, unwilling to accept she could be that vulnerable. Being dead to the world during the daylight hours was bad enough in itself.

"You also moan and whimper. Then your pussy starts creaming, filling the room with your scent."

Another match flared to life while she processed his words. Then the scent of roses complimented the other two candles. "All day long I've kept watch over you, sleeping in short spurts, between bouts of arousal. You called out my name several times, begging me to fuck you."

Anya pulled at her bonds. She couldn't take it. He was too serious for his words to be a lie and she couldn't be that open to anyone. "Don't worry my little vamp, your naughty secret is safe with me. I don't have any intention of telling anyone about your submissive desires."

"Let me go, Cat!" she snarled. Blood lust and sexual heat warred with the need to get as far away from him as fast as she could. A shiver raced down her spine at the desire his words evoked— he was right, she did crave mating with him, his animal nature was a heady draw for her. And that terrified as much as it excited her. She had always settled for flings that were barely lukewarm in an effort to avoid long-term attachment.

His firm hands gripped her ankles as he kneeled on the bed. Sliding his hands up her bare flesh as he moved, he gently caressed her body, like he was afraid of breaking her. It only made her struggle more.

"Relax Anya. I'm not going to hurt you," he soothed. As he moved close enough for her to see his eyes, she gasped. He had gone completely cat, his pupils elongated and dilated.

"I'm not screwing around, Ruben."

His chuckle filled the air moments before he dropped his head and licked at the lips of her sex. A moan of encouragement escaped her lips, causing her to struggle harder, which only made him lap at her pussy, sliding his tongue along her lips.

She wouldn't have thought she could be so ready so quickly. It was almost as if her body had been preparing itself for him while she slept.

"Tell me to stop and I will," he growled as he moved further up her body. Along the way he paused to nip and lick every possible erogenous zone from her hips to her neck. Rather than stop him, she gave in to her body's demands, allowing him to touch as he would. It was only as he settled between her spread thighs, his cock pressing tight against her pussy that she thought to gasp, "I need to feed." As much as she didn't want to end the mood, if she didn't feed before she had sex with him, she might accidentally bite him if he moved his neck too close.

"I know." Ruben dropped his shoulder to rest along her cheek. All she had to do was turn her head and his jugular vein was within biting distance.

Instead, she turned her face away, her body screaming in protest. She had planned to feed from him when they had sex, but he had changed that when he teased her with his blood earlier. To drink again might link them,

"I can't," she managed to gasp out as her hips rocked against his hardness. She could feel her moisture coating her thighs. "Any more of your blood could bind us together, mentally and physically. I've already had it introduced to my system."

Ruben braced himself and lifted his torso off hers, driving his groin tighter against hers. "We are already bound. You're mine, my mate."

His words slammed into her, shattering her views of what the future held for her. She never thought she could make a life with someone and still do what she needed for her people. She also knew shifters took claiming their mates seriously. It wasn't something they casually proclaimed, and with him having all day to think about it, he would know if it was his body or something more crying out for her.

It also caused a curious tingling in her chest to hear him proclaim her as his mate. Never one to believe in fate, it nevertheless felt incredible to know that he was hers, all hers.

"It's not just me, Ruben. I'm a protector, my commitment to my people comes first."

"And mine to my mate takes precedent over all others I might have. Now *feed.*" He dropped his head again and thrust his hips, his cock slipping past her lips, filling her. Unable to resist any longer, she turned her head, pressed her lips tight against his neck in an open mouthed kiss and sank her fangs in.

The sweet tang of his blood flowed into her mouth as he started to move, pumping his hips without dislodging her fangs. Spread-eagle and bound, all she could do was arch her hips up and enjoy his claiming. She had no illusion, that was what he was doing, claiming his mate.

When the hunger for blood was sated, she swirled her tongue over the wound then pulled away, and kissed his cheek, encouraging him to turn his head. Their lips met and she kissed him with all her pent up need from years of loneliness.

The feel of his weight over her thrilled her like nothing else had. It just felt right. She had the sense she could be at peace with all she had done for her people, so long as she was in his arms. Instinctively, she panicked at the thought.

'Mine. All of you, good and bad.' Ruben's thought washed over her, proving her worry about the link. What flowed after was a mass of emotions; desire, a need to be accepted and loved, and a fear of being rejected. With a start, Anya realized what she was feeling was coming from the man joined so intimately with her.

"Untie me," she gasped out as he surged against her, his thrusts picking up pace as their desires fed each other.

"Break free. It's only a thin rope. I didn't—"

'Ah yeah, squeeze me like that again'

"--want to actually keep you against your will. You could have broken free anytime you really wanted to."

Uncertain what was his voice and what was his thoughts flowing to her, she reacted to both, milking his cock with her slick inner muscles as she jerked her limbs hard, snapping all four ropes at once.

Wrapping her body around him, Anya jerked in a smooth movement, flipping him onto his back. Continuing the motion, she slid over him, straddling him and rejoining them. His hands cupped her hips, guiding her back into rhythm while she caressed her breasts, pinching and tweaking her nipples.

The mating grew frantic as she rocked over him, grinding down and working them both into a frenzy of need. With the uncertainty they were living in, it made her need reach a fevered peak. The moment might be all she had, and she wasn't about to go out with regrets.

Shaking her head at the unwelcome thoughts, she focused on the delicious feel of his cock inside her, rubbing against her sensitive, slick walls with each thrust. Arching her back, she worked herself faster, savoring the sounds of his groans echoing off the walls, mingling with her whimpers and gasps of pleasure.

She had had sex before, but it never felt like her body was about to fly apart at the seams. Dropping one of her hands to his chest, she tipped forward, her motions jerky as her body tightened, waves of orgasm crashing through her. Screaming out his name, she dropped her other hand to his chest, trying to milk the last drop of pleasure out of her body.

She could feel the surge of his cock inside her as he climaxed, the hot jets of his passion filled her. Closing her eyes, she gave up trying to hold herself above him and collapsed against his chest, her inner muscles clenching him tight as Ruben shuddered.

Panting softly, she sucked air into her deprived lungs. Ruben was in much the same state if his heavy breathing in her ear was any indication. She knew she should move, shift her weight to his side, but all she wanted to do was lay there until her body recovered, and seduce him again.

Softly, at first Ruben's hands rubbed up and down her back and butt, caressing small circles in her sweaty flesh. Anya almost purred at how good it felt as her skin cooled, her nerves sensitive to the lightest brush of his hand.

"We still have a lot of work left to do before the sun rises again." It almost killed her to say it, but her duty to her people had to come first, and Ruben needed to understand that from the beginning.

"I know."

His hands shifted to the back of her head, and he coaxed her head up, and her lips to his. This kiss was softer than the others, but filled with hints of the same passion that had claimed them both moments before. Anya could feel his heart beating against her chest. With a groan muffled by his lips she broke the kiss and rolled away.

"Any more of that and we won't leave this room until next sunset."

* * *

Several hours later, leaning back against the same tree as the night before, Anya studied her newfound partner as he shifted from tiger to human and donned his clothing. Correction—her mate. Although it was still a foreign concept to her, she was doing her best to respect Ruben's ways, as he was trying to respect hers. For a relationship that had come about in less than a day's time, she thought they were both doing well.

"What do we do if we don't find out who else is involved?"

Ruben's gaze turned toward hers, his eyes still faintly glowing in the dim light. "We go on as we did before, but with the knowledge that there is a potential threat out there. In essence, we learn from Kali and her kind."

"How so?"

Ruben moved closer, leaning his back against the same tree as Anya, his shoulder barely brushing against hers with each breath he took. "Unlike us, humans live such fragile existences, but they keep going. We can't let fear paralyze us.

Riordan survived what was done to him, and if it comes down to it, others will as well."

Anya nodded. "Yet we don't know how many others there were before him. Some of my kind just disappear occasionally, choosing to go off and die as they will it."

Ruben's hand clasped hers, his fingers tangling with hers. He gave it a gentle squeeze and they lapsed into silence. Anya sighed again and returned her focus to scanning the area. Ruben gently squeezed her hand again, and a zing of awareness shot throughout her body. Already she was counting the minutes until they could head back in for the night.

That fate wasn't in her future any more, to go off on her own and die. Now she had something, and someone, to live for.

NATURE OF THE BEAST

Once the last of the council members left the chamber, Kathlyn made her way to her inner sanctum. She settled herself into her chair and stared into space. Time passed slowly as she waited for confirmation that the threat to her people had been removed. Although, she didn't suffer the disillusion that they were completely in the clear, she did hope the threat had been significantly diminished. If Dr. Nelson had been willing to allow Kali to perform some of the research, there could be others who held small bits of information, but hopefully like Kali, they had been kept in the dark about the bulk of the research, only allowed to see a small portion of it. Until the council knew for certain however, they were going to have to be careful.

Sighing softly, she ran a slender hand over her mouth, then dropped it into her lap when she felt it trembling. Closing her eyes, she leaned back in her chair and tried to push away her self-doubts. She had only been on the council a few years, and was the first turn-blood to serve her people in that capacity. Many of her people looked up to her, counting on her to prove that turn-bloods were equal to true-bloods.

"M'lady?"

The softly whispered words startled her. She hadn't heard anyone enter. She was too wrapped up in hoping she hadn't done the wrong thing in pushing for Dr. Nelson's death rather than his capture.

"Yes?"

"I'm sorry to bother you Lady Kathlyn, but I was told to inform you when the deed has been done."

Kathlyn nodded, then forced herself to sound calm. "Thank you. Please make sure I'm not disturbed."

As the door closed behind the messenger, Kathlyn leaned forward, propping her elbows on the table and rested her head in her hands. Closing her eyes, she allowed tears to fall. Not for the death of the doctor, but for Riordan and Kali. If she had pushed harder when Riordan had first come to them with his suspicions, if she had made the other councilors see reason, all that he and his chosen had suffered wouldn't have happened. So much lost time. And there was no telling how many others had been affected, had died in the doctor's lab.

It was some time later when she felt presentable enough to leave the chamber. Pulling the huge doors open was always difficult, but she was weak with hunger, making it more so. She was on her way down the hall to feed when Anya stepped in front of her, a strange man right behind her. Kathlyn stopped. "Yes?"

"M'lady, this is Ruben. He was doing some scouting for his family. It seems the doctor was also trying to grab shifters and Ruben's sister was almost taken."

"Have the other council members been informed?"

"No M'lady. I thought it best to report to you first."

Kathlyn reached out slowly and brushed a strand of Anya's hair out of her eyes. The younger vampire offered a tentative smile in response. The line between protectors and council had always been thin, but sacrosanct. Protectors did not initiate contact with the council, unless it was to protect them. The council was viewed as untouchable, as the elite. However, the addition of the first turn-blood was quickly changing that.

Her relationship to Anya had always been different. Anya's father had turned her, after she had saved the girl's life when she was only a few years old, nearly dying the process. They had learned about being a vampire together, although Anya was almost thirty years her junior.

"Thank you, Anya. You've served our people well. Now I have to ask another favor of you."

"Anything, M'lady." Once it had been Kathlyn, or Kathe when she was just learning to speak. She pushed away the sadness of the changes that had fallen between them and focused her attention on the job she had been brought into the council to do.

"Please inform the other councilors it's time for us to have a meeting with the shifters."

Anya nodded her understanding, and without another word, Kathlyn turned and headed back into the council chambers. It was going to be a long night, and she wanted to sit and rest before the inevitable chaos of hell breaking loose.

* * *

Her first sight of him had Kathlyn drawing in a quick breath of surprise. When the shifters that lived nearby had started arriving, she had marveled at the fluid beauty of their movements. She had met a few of their kind over the years, but had never seen so many in one room.

This one though had a barely leashed intensity that made her pulse quicken. Every movement he took rippled his muscles under his tight jeans and black T-shirt. Unlike the vampires in the room who were dressed in almost formal wear, the shifters had elected to dress casually. She suspected each of them was more comfortable in their relaxed clothing than she was in her ornate gown. The corset underneath was drawn so tight, if she had needed to breathe like a mortal, she would have long since passed out from lack of oxygen.

"Lady Kathlyn, may I present to you Vance, the next alpha of his family."

Out of habit, Kathlyn extended her hand to the stranger after the introduction offered by her aide. As his warm hand closed over hers, her gut clenched with the need to feed, and something more elemental. She wanted this man, this shifter she didn't even know.

"It's a pleasure to meet you, M'lady, although one could wish for better circumstances." Kathlyn flushed at the masculine appraisal in his gaze. He was mentally undressing her, and judging by the sudden elongation of his pupils and the flaring of his nostrils, he liked what he was imagining.

One of the council elders moved to stand next to her and Kathlyn reluctantly dropped Vance's hand, dividing her attention between the two men. As the elder's words registered, she gasped in surprise.

"You want me to take a shifter as my protector? What of my guards?"

"At night they will still attend to you, but we have worked out an agreement with the shifters, to join forces with them, including partnering up to make sure we are not vulnerable during the light of day."

"For how long?" Kathlyn wanted to run a hand through her perfectly braided hair, but tamped down the urge. As a councilor, she had been forced to understand, could not show uncertainly or hesitation in any way in front of those not on the council.

"That we do not yet know. We are thinking a month at most, while we use the information Anya and Kali have compiled to track down the other lab technicians and make sure they are not a threat."

"I see. And why was I not consulted?"

The council elder drew in a sharp inhalation at Kathlyn's audacity to take him to task in front of an outsider, but she was long past caring about protocols. They had ignored her in the past, and one of their kind had had to go to extreme lengths to prove a threat existed. Now it seemed they were back to their old way of doing things, viewing one who had been turned rather than born vampire as inferior. It was a flaw in the council that had caused many problems in the past, given that almost a fourth of their population was turn-bloods rather then true-bloods.

"You were unavailable at the time."

Kathlyn gritted her teeth to keep from retorting that the only time she had been unavailable all night was when she had been feeding, and that had never stopped any of the councilors before. Even then, she had been out for five to ten minutes, hardly enough time for them to have argued and reached an agreement.

"I see. And who has been selected for me, to be my stand-in guard?"

Despite the politeness of her words, Kathlyn allowed a bit of bite into them. The other vampire narrowed his eyes at her, but couldn't say anything without committing the same slight he was upset with her for performing. Inside, Kathlyn allowed herself to smile. Any mistakes she made could be chalked up to her still learning to be without emotion in front of others. The same could not be said for the elder.

"This one here, Vance, has been selected. As the youngest of us, and the weakest, we thought it fitting to have an alpha to watch over you."

Kathlyn felt her smile turn to a sneer at his words, but the idea of being alone with the shifter sent a bolt of pleasure coursing through her. The councilors thought they were slighting her, making her seem weaker in front of the others, but in that moment she didn't care. She was going to be spending time, a lot of time, with the fascinating man beside her.

"Very well, shall we begin the meeting?"

* * *

It was almost daybreak before the meeting finally ended, and Kathlyn had a moment to speak privately with Anya. As soon as the younger vampire left, she turned to her new guardian.

"I know you must have questions. But the sun is about to rise, and I am not yet old enough to fight its pull to sleep, for more than the few minutes it will take to reach my quarters."

Vance smiled, his soft lips curling, the barest hint of teeth flashing at her. Kathlyn inhaled deeply, savoring his outdoorsy musk. Unlike her kind, who often tended to have little to no smell at all, his scent was fresh, and intoxicating.

"I can wait until you're well rested. Although, from the look in your eyes, you need to feed before you sleep."

"Are you offering?" As soon as she said the words she wished she could bring them back. Not that the idea of feeding from the shifter wasn't enticing, but it was the confrontational tone she used that made her cringe. She sounded almost shrewish, and he had done nothing to deserve her temper with the council being taken out on him.

Yet rather than take affront as one of her kind would, he smiled a slow, toe-curling smile. The briefest hint of teeth flashed at her, and his gaze became calculating. "I could be convinced, if I get to do my own biting afterward."

Kathlyn couldn't control the shiver coursing through her at the tempting imagery that sprang to mind. She could almost feel the glide of his skin against her as he covered her, pressing her into the silken sheets of her bed, while his lips traced down the column of her throat.

"As temping as the idea is, I must demure. It is inappropriate for a council member to pursue an intimate relationship with his or her protector." Vance's smile widened at her words. A spark of masculine mischief lit up his dark eyes, until she could feel herself wanting to drown in them. Shaking her head at herself, Kathlyn turned on her heels and walked down the hallway, the sound of his footsteps following hers, echoing against the stone walls.

* * *

Over the next few days she had come to several conclusions. First, the council was trying to drive her insane—or at least some of its members were. The eldest among them had quietly retired two days after the meeting and subsequent alliance with the shifters. Riordan was elected to take his place, as many had thought it should be, and so far he was the only one she knew she could count on to listen to her.

The second, and possibly most distracting conclusion she had arrived at, was that she wanted Vance with a passion she hadn't experienced before. It was slowing making her mad with need. She could feel the air shifting around her with every movement he made. She had become hyper-sensitive, nearly able to feel his moods, and knew he wasn't happy with her denying him.

He had made it clear that although she had managed to avoid falling for his subtle seduction over the last few days, he did expect her to fall into his arms soon. She woke every evening, just as the sun slipped below the horizon, with the scent of his desire wrapping over her.

He insisted on being in the room with her when she slept, and sometime after oblivion claimed her, he would climb into bed with her and wrap himself around her. Thankfully he was clothed, barely.

Brushing her hand over her face, she tried to ignore the way his scent clung to her, masking the slight smell that was her own.

"Kathlyn, are you listening?"

She jerked her head up and stared at the elder councilor, a polite smile curving her lips. Nodding her head, she turned her attention back to the information in front of her. In just a few days they had managed to track down most of Dr. Nelson's former employees and contacts he had used to procure specimens. Only two had had any idea of what the doctor was doing, and they had been dealt with.

As the council droned on, Kathlyn lost herself in her thoughts again. It wasn't until Riordan politely elbowed her that she realized the meeting had been adjourned and everyone was leaving. Flushing scarlet, she turned away from his knowing look. As much as she admired the other vampire, she sometimes felt as if he saw too much.

Gathering her things, she headed out of the room as quickly as she could, and brushed past Vance, knowing he would quickly catch up to her. She could hear the brush of his jeans as he pushed off of the wall he had been leaning against and stalked down the hall after her. She pushed open the door to her chambers and moved to shut it between them, but he slid his foot between the door and its frame, forcing it back open.

"It's not yet time for me to retire and I didn't invite you into my chamber."

His eyes seemed to catch everything as she nervously set the packet of information on her desk and turned to face him, her hands grasping the lip of the desk until they ached with the pressure.

He arched a dark brow at her, and moved closer, a wolf stalking its prey. "Ah Kathlyn, there is so much you need to learn about us shifters that I don't know where to begin. We take our oaths very seriously, and mine is to protect you, for however long you might be in need of my protection. And while I understand I cannot attend council sessions, I will continue to be your shadow elsewhere."

"Damn you," she hissed, frustrated with his attitude. He was like all the other males, and therefore thought he knew what was best. She was sick of it. His constant attempts of seduction weren't helping her mood either. She wasn't used to being touched, and he seemed to do it as often as he could.

Every touch, from the stroke of his fingers down her arm as he helped her out of her chair, to the heat of his palm against her back as he escorted her down the hallways, were all ways of trying to bend her to his will, and she was tired of it. She wasn't even going to think about how she woke with her face pressed against his chest, her legs tangled with his, let alone her deep need for him.

"I didn't ask for your company and I don't appreciate having to constantly be on guard against you."

He took a step back and for a brief moment, she felt ashamed of her overreaction. Despite his continued efforts to persuade her to be intimate with him, he had been nothing but polite and considerate to her. By the gods, he had even listened to her plans for her people, and shared his own ideas for when he took over his pack.

If only he had been vampire and not assigned to protect her, he would be perfect. "Look Vance. I'm...sorry. I know you, as well as your family, are trying to help us. Trust me, I sleep better knowing you are here to watch over me. But for a councilor to sleep with her guard is just not done. It makes her protector susceptible to overlooking things, and letting down his guard. You know that's a dangerous risk, for both of them."

Vance stepped forward and grasped her upper arms in his hands. She could feel the rough pads on his skin, testament to his animal within. "I am not a vampire, Kathlyn. Your guards might operate better at a distance, but for a werewolf, being with someone makes us more protective of their well-being. When we mate, it is a commitment to protect that person—even to the death."

His hands slid slowly up and down her arms, his thumbs stroking tiny circles on her inner arms, igniting her sensitive flesh. She drew in her breath as his knuckles skimmed the undersides of her breasts as he slid his touch higher, then back down.

"I still don't think this is a good idea."

"Then stop thinking," he retorted before tipping his head down and pressing his lips against hers. Instinctively, she wrapped her arms around his neck and held on. The intensity of his kiss mashed her lips as he pulled her tight into his embrace, claiming her mouth with his lips, his tongue, while holding her immobile against him. Kathlyn could have melted at the heat coming off him, but found it intoxicating.

He was taking what he wanted, but at the moment, she didn't care. She forgot her recriminations of moments past, damning men for having to be right. She couldn't even remember why she had denied herself something that felt incredible.

When Vance swept her into his arms, she tightened her hold and refused to break the kiss. The slide of his tongue against hers brought out her fangs, and she grew light-headed as he stroked the velvet heat of his tongue over them.

Laying her on the bed, he came down over her, his hands grasping at the lace stays of her gown. She couldn't hold back a shiver. His mouth never left her as he tried unsuccessfully to undo her gown. She felt the brush of a sharp nail against her skin as he ripped through the laces.

He growled softly into her mouth, and it was the most beautiful sound she had ever heard, and felt. Impatient to feel his skin against hers, she pulled at his shirt and when he wouldn't break the kiss for her to pull it over his head, she ripped it apart.

The intensity of their emotions robbed Kathlyn of rational thought, her only goal to feel the silken heat of his bare flesh against hers, to allow him to claim her as her body was demanding he do.

It was unlike anything she'd ever experienced. Vampires mated with passion, but shifters, at least this one, transcended that. She could feel her toes tingling, and all he had done was kiss her.

As Vance pressed closer, his heart beating rapidly against her breast, Kathlyn pulled back and nipped at his lower lip. With a growl, he thrust it between her teeth and she tasted the metallic sweetness of his blood.

It was just a few drops, before recognition sank in and she pulled back. Gasping for breath, she arched her back and pressed her aching breasts against the light covering of hair on his chest. She thought he would have had more hair, but found that the light dusting was more appealing to her that a full pelt would have been.

Vance moved away from her, shifting on the bed until he knelt beside her. His chest gleamed in the moonlight, tanned skin glistening with a sheen of sweat, muscles flexing as he fought to control his animalistic urges.

'*You're mine.*' Kathlyn's eyes widened at the calm declaration to his words. He wasn't asking, he wasn't staking a claim, he was simply stating something he believed a certainty. Her heart leaped in response, and a need to repeat his words called from somewhere within her soul.

'*And you're mine.*'

Vance's gaze took on a predatory gleam at her words, tracing over the corset that hugged her curves, and forced her generous breasts upward until they almost spilled over the top. He reached out and ripped the cloth away, baring her breasts to his gaze, leaving the rest wrapped tightly around her body.

She could feel her chest rising with each breath, her nipples hard, craving his touch. Almost reverently, he reached out and slid her panties down her legs and tossed them across the room. Then he rolled off the bed, his hands going to the zipper of his jeans.

Kathlyn's eyes focused on the tempting arrow of hair that lead to his groin as it slowly came into view, turning into a thick mat surrounding his cock. He was hard, and thick, the head a dusky red. She could see the vein throbbing, and felt her fangs lengthen again, craving more of the sweetness of his blood.

She wanted to close her eyes, to shut out the temptation, but found him too beautiful to deny herself the pleasure. As he stepped from of the last of his clothing and rejoined her on the bed, Kathlyn held out her arms, expecting him to settle back into her embrace. Instead, he pulled the pillows from the head of the bed and plumped them together next to her hip.

"Roll over," he growled, sensuality lacing his tone. She could smell the mingling of their scents in the air. Uncertain what he wanted of her, but knowing she couldn't survive long without more of his touch, she rolled over onto the pillow, her ass arching into the air.

She gasped as she felt him move in behind her, the firm heat of his legs settling between hers, pushing her thighs wider apart. His hands brushed her breasts as he positioned the pillows under her, until she could rest comfortably upon them. She had tried the position as a mortal, and found it somewhat lacking, but as Vance shifted closer, his cock rubbing against the slit of her pussy, she realized it was the lack of passion she had felt for her partner at the time. Her nerves were flaring to life, screaming for the euphoria of release.

Fisting her hands into the silken material covering her pillows, she arched back against him as he cupped her hips and guided his cock between her lips, into her core. She had never imagined wanting to keep her corset on during sex, but with Vance if felt right. So did the molten firmness of his cock as he slid further into her pussy, joining them together as one.

When he started to move it was all Kathlyn could do to keep from screaming her pleasure. Her body was a mass of tangled nerve endings, the feel of his solid warmth against her back making her clit throb, her breasts felt heavier with each glide of his body in and out of hers.

His arms brushed against hers as he released his hold on one hip and braced his palm on the bed next to her cheek. She watched a vein in his forearm throb with each beat of his heart as he thrust into her, working them both hard toward the sweet bliss that beckoned. When he shifted his other hand around her body, and stroked her clit, she turned her head and sank her teeth into his arm, unable to deny herself any longer.

Vance growled, his body jerking hard against hers, momentarily forcing him out of rhythm, but as his blood flowed into her mouth, he glided back into it. The sound of their flesh slamming together, the smell of their mingled essences, the feel of his body moving against hers, claiming her, and finally the taste of his life's blood flowing into her mouth was the aphrodisiac her long denied body needed. She closed her eyes, and tiny sparks danced behind her closed lids as she awakened in a rush, drowning her in sensations until she threw back her head and screamed out her orgasm.

Vance's body jerked hard, then a second time, and she could feel the molten flow of his release flooding her, filling her body with the result of their shared passion. His fingers continued to stroke and pluck at her clit as his hips rocked against hers, and she surrendered to his touch again, trembling with the intensity of her response to him.

He collapsed against her, the weight of his body not enough to hurt her, but enough to have an emotional impact. She felt claimed, her body held still beneath his as his breathing slowed and his pulse returned to normal.

Swirling her tongue over the punctures in his arm, she coaxed another groan from Vance.

'*Mine,*' he thought, and she heard it whisper across her mind. '*My mate.*' As the meaning of his words settled in her mind, she couldn't help responding in kind, '*As I am yours.*'

Vance's soft growl of approval echoed off the walls, and despite the threat to her people, despite her seemingly unending battle with the council, Kathlyn felt hope. In his arms she was safe, and they could figure it out together. She knew enough of shifters to know they took seriously the declaration of mating, and rather than be scared of what it meant, she felt reassured. For the first time since being turned, she felt as if she belonged.

Everything else would be figured out in its own time.

ABOUT THE AUTHOR

Born to ride on the back of dragons, to journey among the stars in a ship traveling faster than light, or to dance the night away in the arms of a mysterious vampire, Michelle Houston willingly shares the worlds in her mind in an effort to bring them to life.

Writing everything from short and sweet stories, to hot and spicy tales of kink, from contemporary tales of romance to erotic romances featuring Greek gods, vampires and were-creatures, she has crossed sexualities and has gone wherever her mental muse has guided her, a journey she has never regretted.

Beyond that, she has a love of the natural world around us (except for insects, spiders, snakes, scorpions, and jellyfish, and she reserves the right to add more at any time).

In other words, she is an ordinary woman with an imagination that is only held in bounds by how fast she can type.

You can find out more about Michelle Houston on her website at: www.michellehouston.com

www.ingramcontent.com/pod-product-compliance
Lightning Source LLC
Chambersburg PA
CBHW071250130626
46556CB00003B/1254